TOAD DELIGHT

MORRIS GLEITZMAN

PUFFIN

PUFFIN BOOKS

UK | USA | Canada | Ireland | Australia
India | New Zealand | South Africa

Puffin Books is part of the Penguin Random House group of companies
whose addresses can be found at global.penguinrandomhouse.com.

www.penguin.co.uk
www.puffin.co.uk
www.ladybird.co.uk

Penguin
Random House
UK

First published by Penguin Random House Australia 2016
Published in Great Britain by Puffin Books 2017

001

Text copyright © Morris Gleitzman, 2016

The moral right of the author has been asserted

Internal design by Tony Palmer
Typeset in 13/15pt Minion Regular
Printed in Great Britain by Clays Ltd, St Ives plc

A CIP catalogue record for this book is available from the British Library

ISBN: 978-0-141-37524-3

All correspondence to:
Puffin Books,
Penguin Random House Children's,
80 Strand, London WC2R 0RL

For Pam

1

The early-morning sun twinkled cheerfully through the swamp.

Limpy tried to ignore it.

Dopey sun. This wasn't the time for cheerful twinkling. Didn't the sun know a very sad moment when it saw one?

Clearly not.

Limpy hopped onto the highway and over to Uncle Spencer.

'Oo-roo, Uncle Spencer,' said Limpy quietly.

Uncle Spencer didn't reply.

Limpy wasn't surprised.

He'd been saying goodbye to rellies for most of his life, and not once had an uncle replied, 'And oo-roo to you too, young Limpy.'

Limpy didn't take it personally. Uncle Spencer and the others couldn't help it. They weren't unfriendly. Or grumpy.

Just flat.

With a sigh, Limpy hopped slowly along the highway to his next squashed rellie.

'Bye, Aunty Sasha,' he said.

'Tragic,' croaked a voice.

Limpy peered more closely at Aunty Sasha in case she was a bit less squashed and a bit less dead than she looked.

But Aunty Sasha, who'd loved a chat when she was alive, wasn't moving a wart or making a sound. Her chatting days, Limpy saw sadly, were behind her. Along with her mouth, which was squished into her own bottom.

Limpy turned and squinted back at Uncle Spencer. Uncle Spencer wasn't saying anything either. He couldn't, not with tyre tracks across his vocal chords, which were poking out of his ears.

'Still,' said the voice. 'Could be worse. At least they died happy.'

The voice, Limpy realised, belonged to a goanna who was perched on a branch, looking down at the dead rellies thoughtfully.

Limpy glared at the goanna.

Rude reptile, butting in and making comments about somebody else's family tragedies.

Except, Limpy had to admit, the goanna was right. Uncle Spencer did look like he'd died happy.

Part of a roadside ants' nest was poking out of Uncle Spencer's mouth, and Uncle Spencer always said there was nothing as delicious as ants in their own home. Except stinkweed with mould on it, and in both of Uncle Spencer's fists were bunches of stinkweed dotted with mould and dazed ants not able to believe their luck.

Oh well, thought Limpy, at least Uncle Spencer's last meal was his favourite.

There were clues that Aunty Sasha had died happy too. Limpy could see traces of honey, which she loved, in her armpits. And an entire wild honeybees' nest, with its roadside branch still attached, clutched to her chest.

Limpy was glad for both of them.

But at the same time he wasn't.

'I've been watching you, young fella,' said the goanna to Limpy. 'Don't miss a morning down here at wart central, do you? Oo-rooing the placemats and trying to figure out why humans hate you lot so much. Have you worked it out yet?'

'I don't want to talk about it,' said Limpy.

He didn't mean to sound unfriendly, but it was a very sensitive subject.

'Wish you'd hurry up and find out,' said the goanna. 'Those humans are a menace to the rest of us, ignoring the road rules and swerving all over the place trying to flatten you lot. Number of times I've nearly been hit myself. Mostly by flying cane toad parts.'

Limpy took a deep breath through his skin pores and tried not to get cross.

'I'm doing my best,' he said to the goanna. 'It's not easy.'

'Let's see if I can give you a few hints,' said the goanna, settling back on the branch. 'OK, off the top of my head, just tossing it in for what it's worth, I reckon humans hate you lot on account of you're so revoltingly ugly.'

Limpy gave the goanna a look.

The goanna was deep in thought.

'And slimy,' it said.

'You're very kind,' said Limpy. 'Lucky for you my cousin Goliath isn't here. If Goliath heard suggestions like that, he'd lose his temper and eat you and half your tree.'

The goanna glanced around, saw that Goliath wasn't there, and went back to being thoughtful.

'My theory is it's the warts,' said the goanna. 'Humans hate you lot because you're revoltingly warty and they're scared you'll cuddle their babies and give them warts too.'

'Nice talking to you,' said Limpy. 'Please don't think I'm being rude, but my family needs me.'

He headed off along the highway to see if any other rellies had been run over.

'Plus,' called out the goanna, 'there's the whole pet thing. Humans have had a gutful of you lot eating their pets. And their washing.'

Limpy hurried away, wishing the goanna would be quiet.

'Hang on,' yelled the goanna. 'I've got another theory. Humans hate you cane toads because you're greedy and cold-blooded without a warm sensitive

4

feeling or emotion in your whole body. Just tossing it in for what it's worth.'

Limpy sighed.

That was ridiculous.

The goanna was totally and completely wrong about cane toads not having sensitive feelings.

Mum and Dad and the others had heaps of sensitive feelings. That was the problem.

If it wasn't for their sensitive and easily hurt feelings, Limpy could come out with it. Tell them he knew exactly why humans hated them.

For weeks he'd been trying to squeeze up the courage to blurt it out, but he hadn't been able to.

It was bad enough that fourteen-tonne trucks wanted to flatten Mum and Dad and the others, without him doing it as well.

2

After Limpy had finished saying goodbye to the squashed rellies, he went to do his other regular morning chore.

Stopping Goliath from getting himself killed.

Each morning, first thing, Goliath liked to spend a bit of time on his favourite hobby.

Threatening traffic.

It was a simple hobby but, as Limpy was always trying to tell Goliath, a very dangerous one.

'Goliath,' he often pleaded. 'Why don't you get a safer hobby, like collecting gumnuts?'

Collecting gumnuts was safer because it didn't involve going onto the highway with a sharpened stick and yelling at human drivers that they were fat bums and poo brains and you were going to stab their petrol tanks and rip their tyres off and stuff their catalytic converters up their turbo pipes.

'He's very brave,' some of the toads murmured now and again about Goliath.

'No he's not,' muttered others. 'He's an idiot.'

Limpy tried to stay somewhere in the middle. But it was hard when the stick-jabber was your favourite cousin.

Sometimes in moments of stress Limpy got a bit exasperated.

'When nature was handing out brains,' he'd yelled at Goliath a few times, 'there must have been a mix-up and you must have got a double-serve of arm muscles and thick skull bones instead.'

Other times he stayed quiet and hoped for Goliath's sake that Mum was right, that it was possible to get smarter if you ate those bugs whose brains were on the outside of their heads.

So far, amazingly, Goliath hadn't been squashed flat even the slightest bit. But Limpy feared it was only a matter of time.

This morning, Limpy was surprised to see that Goliath wasn't at his usual stick-sharpening spot in the swamp clearing.

Strange.

The stick-sharpening rock was still mossy, so Goliath hadn't sharpened any sticks yet. Plus there were no piles of swamp pebbles with the slime sucked off, so Goliath must be having his breakfast somewhere else.

Not, Limpy hoped, in the middle of the highway.

The creepers behind him rustled.

Limpy turned.

It wasn't Goliath.

Limpy was only disappointed for a blink.

'There you are,' said Charm.

Her dear warty face was glowing with pleasure.

Limpy felt the same way. When nature had handed out little sisters, he'd been the luckiest toad in the whole swamp. In the whole northern half of Australia, probably.

They hugged, then Limpy saw that Charm's face was creased with concern.

'What's wrong?' he said.

'Limpy,' she said. 'There's something I want to say. I've been trying to get brave enough to say it for a while, and now I have to. It's about your hobby.'

'Hobby?' said Limpy, puzzled.

'The thing you do every morning,' said Charm. 'Going onto the highway and getting sad about the squashed rellies.'

'I'm saying goodbye to them,' said Limpy quietly.

'You're doing more than that,' said Charm. 'You're fretting and making yourself miserable.'

'No I'm not,' said Limpy. But he heard exactly how he said it.

Miserably.

Charm put her arms round him again. Or tried to. Limpy knew the main reason she wished she was full-sized was so she could get her arms all the way round each member of the family.

He knew exactly how she felt.

If his crook leg wasn't so crook, he'd be better at protecting each member of the family.

'Limpy,' said Charm. 'You've tried so hard to find out why humans want to kill us. You've been a hero at that. But please stop torturing yourself. Just accept that humans hate us and they always will. I want my happy brother back. We used to have so much fun, remember?'

Limpy looked at Charm's earnest loving face.

He could sort of remember a mud slide and Dad blowing up balloons that were really those slime maggots who have their bladders on the outside. But that was it. Just a few faint memories. He couldn't even fully remember what fun felt like.

'I think I know why humans hate us,' he said.

He hadn't planned to say that, and when he saw Charm's eyes get bigger with curiosity and concern, he wished he hadn't.

Except part of him wanted to tell her now, just blurt it out.

He didn't.

Before saying something so upsetting, he had to be totally sure.

'I just need a bit more time,' he said.

Charm's face went into a pout.

'That's what you always say,' she muttered.

She wouldn't be pulling that sulky face, thought Limpy, if she knew what it'll mean if I'm right. How hard it'll be. How different we'll all have to be. How much about ourselves we'll have to change.

Limpy tried to imagine Goliath changing even a tiny bit.

He couldn't.

Goliath didn't even like changing the words he yelled at cars. Fat. Bums. Stab. Turbo pipes. They were the same every time.

'Where is Goliath?' said Limpy.

Charm looked at him as if he was a bit dopey.

'Haven't you heard?' she said.

'What?' said Limpy.

'The whole swamp's talking about it,' said Charm. 'Goliath's fallen in love.'

3

Limpy crouched in the undergrowth and stared into the grotto, stunned.

'Stack me,' he whispered.

There weren't many grottoes in the swamp. Limpy had heard rumours about them, so he guessed this was one. It had a soft carpet of bright green moss and a curved roof of tangled creepers. But it wasn't the grotto that was making Limpy feel stunned.

It was Goliath.

He was sitting on a mound of freshly picked waterlilies. His big muscly arm was round someone else. He was gazing adoringly at her and murmuring softly into her ear.

Limpy couldn't believe it.

Goliath?

The bloke who usually wiped his mouth on a stinkweed leaf after kissing a relative?

In love?

Limpy realised his own mouth was hanging open so wide that the clouds of flying insects hovering in front of his face were staring inside nervously.

He shut his mouth and peered more closely at the romantic couple.

Goliath's girlfriend looked sort of familiar, but Limpy couldn't quite place her.

'She's a penguin,' whispered Charm.

Limpy nodded. Charm was right. He'd seen pictures of penguins in the human travel brochures that often ended up in campground rubbish bins.

That's why the girlfriend's big dark eyes, shiny black fur and beautiful yellow beak were familiar. It was her blue zip-up pockets and red plastic straps that were confusing.

Limpy hopped closer, almost into the grotto, to have a better squiz.

Goliath's girlfriend didn't just have pockets and straps, Limpy saw. She also had a drink holder and a place for a name tag.

He realised why.

'She's a backpack,' Limpy whispered to Charm, horrified. 'Goliath's fallen in love with a penguin backpack.'

'Isn't it wonderful?' said Charm. 'I'm so glad for Goliath. Look how much they adore each other.'

Limpy could barely speak.

'Backpacks can't adore anyone,' he croaked. 'Backpacks don't have feelings, just zips.'

Charm was looking at him sternly.

'You're being very negative,' she said. 'I think you've been spending too much time on the highway.'

Limpy wanted to be glad for Goliath, but it was impossible. All he could think of was Goliath with a broken heart and possibly a finger caught in a zip.

Before Charm could stop him, Limpy hopped into the grotto.

'Goliath,' he whispered urgently. 'Can I have a word with you?'

Goliath looked up and his big warty face beamed.

'Limpy,' he said. 'Great to see you. Penny, this is my cousin Limpy. Limpy, this is Penny.'

Goliath leaned forward.

'Isn't she gorgeous?' he whispered to Limpy. 'She's the most beautiful fully insulated school lunch backpack I've ever met.'

Limpy wasn't sure what to say.

He didn't want to be rude.

'Hello, Penny,' he mumbled. 'Goliath, can we have a little chat?'

Goliath, glowing with love, didn't seem to hear.

'And she's so generous,' he said, kissing Penny's plastic cheek. 'All she wants to do is make me happy.'

He unzipped her main section, reached inside, pulled out a cheese stick and munched it happily.

'Goliath,' hissed Limpy.

Goliath leaned towards him again.

'She loves me just as much as I love her,' whispered Goliath. 'When I told her I can fit four

13

lizards and a section of brake lining in my mouth all at once, she was so impressed.'

Limpy grabbed Goliath's big shoulders.

'Goliath,' he said. 'She's a backpack.'

'I know,' said Goliath dreamily. 'I still can't believe how lucky I am.'

'Limpy,' hissed another voice urgently.

It was Charm. Limpy assumed she was going to give him a lecture on being negative.

Until he turned and saw her fearful face, and what she was pointing at.

Striding towards them, crashing through the undergrowth, were three humans.

Two of the humans were adults, a male and a female. The female was filming Goliath with her mobile phone.

For a fleeting moment, Limpy thought this might be a good thing. A chance for humans to see cane toads at their best. Romantic, loving and very good at arranging waterlilies.

He quickly realised it wasn't a good thing.

Both the human adults had red scrunched-up faces, which Limpy knew meant they were angry. Plus he could see their teeth, which he knew meant they were very angry.

The male was clutching a cricket bat in one hand and the hand of a little human girl in the other. The girl was making sad noises and doing the watery thing with her eyes that humans did when they were upset.

The female, still filming, reached up and broke a dead branch off a tree and gripped it like a weapon.

Limpy's warts trembled.

The humans were almost at the grotto, glaring at Goliath and Penny.

'Hop for it,' croaked Limpy.

Too late.

The adult female swung the branch and flattened the grotto.

'Goliath,' croaked Limpy.

But the tangled wreckage started to move, and Goliath struggled out of it, glaring at the humans, his arm still round Penny.

'Mongrels,' croaked Goliath.

Limpy saw this wasn't going to end in a good way.

He grabbed Charm, who was already on her way to rescue Goliath, and pushed her into the undergrowth, out of sight.

'No,' she said, 'Goliath needs us.'

Limpy agreed. But little sisters tragically kept half-sized by pollution were no match for angry humans with full-sized cricket bats.

'Stay here,' said Limpy. 'You and me are all that Mum and Dad have got left. One of us has to be around for them.'

Charm frowned, but she didn't argue. Limpy was grateful. Usually at moments like this they had arguments about which would get them in the poo quickest, her size or his leg.

Limpy went to save Goliath.

Goliath didn't look interested in being saved.

He was hanging on to Penny's strap with all his strength while the female adult human waved Penny over her head, trying to fling him off.

'You nasty mean selfish brute,' the female adult was yelling. 'Upsetting an innocent child. Let go, you greedy selfish monster.'

Limpy couldn't understand the words, but he could see that the female adult wasn't falling in love with Goliath, not even a little bit.

'Goliath,' he croaked. 'You have to let Penny go. Let her go, Goliath. There'll be other backpacks. You'll love again, I promise.'

Too late.

The adult male swung the cricket bat and Limpy watched in horror as it smacked into Goliath's tummy and the wailing Goliath hurtled high into the air and off into the far distance.

Limpy ducked behind a bush.

This was partly to give the humans a chance to inspect Penny, then return her to the tearful girl, then all stamp away still muttering. But it was also to wait till his tummy stopped having the cramp spasms he got sometimes when he feared Goliath or Charm might be dead.

As soon as the spasms ended, Limpy and Charm went to find Goliath.

He was a long way away, but they found him easily from his sobs and howls in the distance.

'Penny,' he was wailing. 'Come back to me.'

'Is anything broken?' Limpy anxiously asked Goliath when they got there.

'Just his heart,' said Charm sadly.

They helped Goliath down from the prickle bush he'd landed in. Goliath had lots of prickles sticking out of his big warts, but he didn't seem to be feeling any of them.

'Penny,' he moaned. 'I want Penny.'

Charm hugged him between the prickles, then started carefully removing them one by one.

'You'll get over her,' she said. 'You will. You'll meet a lovely picnic hamper and forget all about her.'

'I won't,' wailed Goliath. 'I want Penny. She's mine.'

Limpy's warts drooped for Goliath.

They drooped for another reason as well. Limpy couldn't stop thinking about the things the angry female human had been yelling.

He hadn't understood her words, but her body language had said it all.

Goliath, she'd been saying, was a mean nasty greedy selfish monster.

And she had the movie on her phone to prove it. A movie that soon humans everywhere would be sharing. Limpy had seen in campgrounds how much humans liked looking at things on their phones, specially when they were queueing for a shower or cooking chops.

This was everything Limpy had feared.

If this was how humans felt, no wonder they didn't mind wearing out their tyres and putting stress on their cricket bats to get rid of cane toads.

Limpy couldn't stay silent any longer.

He had to tell somebody.

4

Ancient Abigail didn't look pleased to see Limpy.

'What do you want?' she demanded through a mouthful of lizard burger.

'Um,' said Limpy nervously. 'I need to ask you something. On account of you being the oldest and wisest toad in the swamp.'

He decided not to say, 'and because you get this big mud cave to live in and all the food you can eat in return for sharing your wisdom.' That might have sounded rude, and Limpy had heard that Ancient Abigail could be a bit bad-tempered.

Ancient Abigail grunted and slid another lizard burger into her mouth.

'Go on then,' she said, spraying Limpy with lizardy crumbs.

Limpy glanced around the mud cave while he gathered his thoughts.

Ancient Abigail's place was huge.

Which it needed to be, because so was Ancient

Abigail. Limpy had heard that each day she ate more than her own body weight in lizard burgers.

'Well,' said Limpy. 'Um . . .'

Suddenly he wasn't sure how to say it.

'Spit it out,' said Ancient Abigail, spitting out a fair bit herself.

Limpy decided he just had to blurt it out.

'Would you say,' he said, 'in your opinion, that we cane toads are –'

'Hang on,' said Ancient Abigail, pointing. 'Pass me that over there. I always get nervous when a visitor's here and there's only one left.'

Limpy handed her the last lizard burger, which she ate.

'Now, back to your question,' she said. 'Would I say that we cane toads are what?'

Limpy took a deep breath through his skin pores.

'Greedy and selfish,' he said.

Ancient Abigail looked at him for a long time, frowning. Limpy started to understand how a lizard burger might feel.

'How do you mean?' grunted Ancient Abigail. 'Greedy and selfish?'

Limpy also knew how a bog weevil in Goliath's tummy probably felt. With no choice but to keep going, trying not to think about what might happen at the other end.

'Well,' said Limpy, 'we're always hearing how things are getting a bit scarce, right? Water, edible species, the good weather we used to have, stuff like that. And not just here, everywhere. Migrating birds are always going on about it. I'm wondering if the reason humans hate us cane toads is because we're always gobbling up more than we need.'

There was a long silence.

Limpy held his breath, fearing that Ancient Abigail was getting angry.

He hoped desperately she wasn't taking this personally. He hoped she understood that he was talking about all cane toads.

All except her.

Oh no, he thought. I should have said that.

'Hmmmm,' said Ancient Abigail. 'Gobbling up more than we need. I think you might be right.'

Limpy stared at her, surprised and relieved. It was the first time he'd ever heard anybody admit that something was true when they probably didn't want it to be.

This must be what wisdom is, thought Limpy. Everyone said Ancient Abigail had huge amounts of wisdom as well as huge amounts of loose skin behind her knees, and they were right.

'Take a look at this,' said Ancient Abigail.

Limpy was relieved she wasn't talking about her knees.

She was holding out a flat oblong thing with glass on one side.

'It's a tablet,' said Ancient Abigail.

Limpy was puzzled. It didn't look like any tablet

he'd ever seen. He'd only ever seen one, a small pill Goliath had found in the picnic ground, which when Goliath ate it made him poo even more than usual, which was a lot.

'Humans use these to see things,' said Ancient Abigail, tapping the oblong tablet. 'They prefer it to looking around.'

'Where did you get it?' asked Limpy.

'Goliath found it in a human tent,' said Ancient Abigail. 'He thought it was something to eat.'

Limpy noticed that one corner did look a bit chewed.

Ancient Abigail pressed something on the edge of the tablet and suddenly the glass side came to life.

Limpy took a step back.

Then he realised he'd seen something like this before, in a human campervan. The tablet was like a big phone. Being bigger probably made it break less easily when the humans gawking at it walked into trees.

'Have to be quick,' said Ancient Abigail. 'Not much battery left.'

She signalled for Limpy to look more closely at the coloured images moving on the tablet.

He did.

And blinked with shock.

On the screen were cane toads, lots of different ones in lots of different places. But they all had one thing in common.

They were stuffing things into their mouths, often several at a time.

Groceries, shoes, small pets, car parts, garden ornaments, lots of the produce of vegetable farms, and quite a few barbecue heat beads. And huge numbers of other bush creatures, including dead kangaroos on the highway even though they could only get one foot in.

'Is this what you mean?' asked Ancient Abigail.

Limpy nodded.

After a while the screen showed a map. Limpy knew it was a map of Australia because he'd seen it on campervan stickers and drivers' tattoos.

The top half of the map was covered with little cane toad figures moving down towards the bottom of the map like an advancing army. Suddenly diagonal red crosses appeared, slashing across the cane toads.

Limpy knew what diagonal red crosses meant. He'd seen plenty of them on signs in caravan parks.

Forbidden.

Not Wanted.

Get Rid Of.

Stamp Out.

The tablet screen went blank.

'Battery's conked,' said Ancient Abigail.

Limpy was dizzy with alarm. It was worse than his worst nightmares, even the ones he'd had after Goliath had persuaded him to try some barbecue heat beads.

'We have to warn the others,' Limpy croaked to Ancient Abigail. 'Tell them that if we don't stop being greedy with food and other creatures and barbecue accessories, the humans will kill us all.'

Ancient Abigail thought about this.

'You're probably right, young Limpy,' she said. 'But here's the rub. In my long experience, if you tell other folk things they don't want to hear, maybe even things they find a bit insulting and hurtful, they can be very stingy with, oh, I don't know, lizard burgers for example.'

Limpy stared at Ancient Abigail, who was picking lizard crumbs off her front and didn't seem to want to look him in the eye.

'But somebody's got to tell them,' said Limpy. 'Somebody's got to.'

Suddenly Ancient Abigail was looking at him.

Right at him.

From outside the mud cave came the sound of heavy hopping and a lot of croaking.

'Sorry,' said Ancient Abigail to Limpy. 'Bit busy right now.'

She turned to the entrance and gave a yell.

'In here, boys.'

Several of Limpy's second and third cousins came in, dragging big swamp leaves piled with burgers.

Ancient Abigail threw herself into organising where they should be stacked. She seemed to have forgotten Limpy was even there.

But as Limpy hopped outside, his heart heavy and his thoughts full of what he had to do, Ancient Abigail's voice floated out after him.

'Good luck, young fella. Be brave, be strong.'

'Thanks,' said Limpy.

'And eat more,' called Ancient Abigail. 'You need fattening up.'

5

'Greedy?'

Mum looked at Limpy, shocked and hurt.

Limpy sighed.

This was what he'd feared.

'Not just you,' he said hastily. 'All of us. Cane toads everywhere.'

This didn't seem to make Mum feel any better. And on the big leaf where she was preparing dinner, several of the termites and slugs and weevils waiting to be mixed up together and marinated in their own juices looked shocked too.

'That's a bit rough,' said a bog weevil. 'You cane toads have got healthy appetites, sure, that's why we're here today, but greedy, no way.'

'If my son spoke to me like that,' said a termite, 'I'd give him a good talking to. Well, I would if you hadn't eaten him last week.'

Limpy shivered, as if a cold breeze had just touched his warts.

For a moment he assumed it was because of the way Mum and Dad and Charm and quite a lot of their dinner were looking at him. But then his crook leg started to twitch and Limpy knew from experience what that meant.

A storm was coming.

He ignored it. He had a more important storm to deal with, the one that was rumbling in his family.

Dad was frowning so hard that some of his warts had turned inside out.

'Limpy,' he said. 'Mum and I didn't bring you up to carry on with this sort of caper. Hurting the feelings of family members with name-calling.'

Limpy sighed again.

'I'm just trying to help,' he said. 'I'm just saying that the more we understand why humans hate us, the better we can protect ourselves. Humans reckon we're greedy and I can see why. Look at all this dinner, just for the five of us.'

Limpy pointed to the several hundred insects waiting patiently in line.

'Oh, very nice,' said a dung beetle. 'Very hurtful, when we've all made the effort to be here.'

The other insects agreed.

'We've always eaten this much,' said Mum, even more hurt. 'It's normal. Limpy, I thought you appreciated the effort I put into making you nice meals.'

'The effort we all put in,' said Dad.

'Hear, hear,' said the insects.

'Limpy,' said Charm. 'I think you'd better leave this conversation for another time.'

Limpy felt like his warts were going to pop with frustration.

'All I'm suggesting,' he wanted to yell, 'is that we try to eat a little less. Show humans we can be a bit more generous and a bit more sharing. I'm not saying we have to starve ourselves to death. It's not the end of the world.'

Before Limpy could say any of those things, a throat-sac-wobbling crack shook the leaves around them and the air shuddered with a roll of thunder so loud it did sound like the world was ending.

'Storm,' yelled Limpy. 'Everyone under cover.'

They all hurried under the thick leaves of the storm shelter, insects included.

'Where's Goliath?' said Limpy.

He was relieved to see that Goliath was already in there, slumped in a corner next to a large pile of grasshopper husks and snail shells.

'Can you please keep the noise down,' said Goliath. 'I'm nursing a broken heart here.'

His big body drooped some more and didn't stop drooping even when he put a handful of grasshoppers and snails into his mouth.

Limpy was shocked. Usually, no matter how unhappy Goliath was feeling, a big mouthful of food was the one sure way to perk him up.

Poor bloke, thought Limpy sadly, he must really be suffering.

'If you truly want to help this family,' said Dad to Limpy, 'you can start by finding Goliath a new girlfriend.'

'Penny,' whimpered Goliath.

'And,' said Charm, 'perhaps you can give us a bit more warning next time a storm comes. Is your leg having a day off?'

'Now come on,' said Mum. 'Don't all gang up on Limpy. Storm warnings shouldn't be his responsibility. We've got storm beetles for that.'

'Not any more,' said Limpy quietly. 'We've eaten them all.'

Mum and Dad and Charm all glared at him and Limpy could see Charm was right, this conversation should be left for another day.

'For your information,' said Charm, 'we haven't eaten them all. There are two over there.'

Limpy looked to where she was pointing.

She was right.

Two trembling storm beetles were sitting on Goliath's knee.

'Sorry,' said one of storm beetles. 'We should have warned you. But we're exhausted. There's only two of us left in the whole district. We've got to do all the storm warnings, plus all the breeding.'

Before Limpy could suggest to them that perhaps the knee of a lovesick insect gobbler wasn't the best place to start a family, more thunder exploded and violent gusts of wind shook the leaves above them.

And another sound started.

29

A ripping, tearing, shredding sound.

Limpy peered out of the shelter.

And blinked.

Crashing down from the sky was very heavy rain, except it wasn't drops of water, it was small jagged lumps of what looked like glass.

Limpy had never seen anything like it.

For a moment he wondered if a few hundred cars on the highway had smashed into each other in the storm and these were bits of their windscreens raining down.

It didn't seem likely. And the wind was suddenly very cold.

'What's going on?' said Mum.

'Don't know,' said Dad. 'Let's ask the storm beetles.'

They all turned to Goliath. His knee was bare. Goliath was licking his lips. He looked at them guiltily.

'Oops,' he said.

Limpy forced himself not to get cross with a heart-broken cousin.

He turned back to the crashing lumps of rain, which were being flung around the swamp now by the wind.

'I think I know what that is,' said Charm. 'It's what a seagull from down south told me about once. Those are lumps of ice. It's called hail.'

Limpy was stunned.

'Ice?' he croaked.

Mum and Dad looked stunned too.

'This is the tropics,' said Dad. 'The only ice we're meant to have up here is from human ice-cream storage facilities.'

The ripping, tearing, shredding sounds were continuing.

Limpy looked nervously at the roof.

It seemed OK. He was glad that when they'd decided to have a storm shelter on account of all the storms lately, they'd chosen some of the thickest and strongest leaves in the swamp and riveted them together with hookworms.

'Hear all that ripping, tearing and shredding?' said Goliath through a mouthful of the family's dinner. 'That's what's happened to my heart.'

Charm went over and gave him a hug.

Mum and Dad did too.

Limpy decided to hug Goliath later. He stayed staring at the hail. He was having a very troubling thought.

What if it wasn't only humans who'd had a gutful of greedy cane toads?

What if the weather had as well?

6

When the storm was over, Limpy went to check on the rellies. Not the ones on the highway, the ones in his room.

Then he inspected the stack of flat uncles, then he checked the flat aunty stack, then the flat cousin stack.

Phew, what a relief. No hail damage or wind damage to any of them, thanks to the thick leafy hookworm-reinforced ceiling.

Limpy was glad. Poor rellies, they'd suffered enough already, squashed flat on the highway and sun-baked into hard discs with only their surprised faces to remind anyone who they were.

'Limpy.'

He jumped.

Sometimes, lying in bed surrounded by the stacks of rellies, Limpy imagined just before he went to sleep that the rellies were talking to him.

Thanking him for stacking them so neatly.

Begging him to find a way for cane toads to live peacefully with humans before Mum and Dad had to build an extension onto his room for more stacks.

Limpy turned.

The rellies weren't speaking to him now.

It was Mum, with Dad next to her.

'We've come to say sorry,' said Mum quietly. 'We were too hard on you earlier. It did hurt, when you called us selfish, but the way we reacted to it was, well, a bit selfish.'

Dad put his hand on Limpy's shoulder.

'That comment I made about the way we brought you up,' said Dad. 'That wasn't a fair thing to say. You've turned out exactly as we hoped. Only better.'

'Thanks,' said Limpy to both of them.

'When that flood swept away all our other little tadpoles,' said Dad, 'me and Mum thought we were the unluckiest parents in the swamp. But the flood left us with you and Charm, and now we reckon that makes us the luckiest.'

Limpy's throat sac was so wobbly he couldn't speak.

'We're proud of you, Limpy,' said Mum. 'The way you're always trying to protect us cane toads. But love, we are what we are, and we've always been that way. Yes, we probably do eat a bit too much, but every time you and Charm and Goliath hop off for the day, I can't be certain I'm ever going to see you again. Not if humans see you first. So I make every meal as big and special as I can, in case it's the last.'

Limpy stared at Mum's concerned loving face.

He put his arms round her.

'I've never thought of it that way,' he whispered.

'Even if we did go on a diet,' said Dad, 'that's only five of us. Four really, because if Goliath doesn't have a lot of food, he faints. There are huge mobs of cane toads just in this swamp, so what difference would four really make?'

Limpy looked at Dad's earnest loving face.

You've got to start somewhere, that's what Limpy had always told himself.

Now he wasn't so sure.

'What I'm about to say,' said Mum, 'is hard to hear, I know that. But love, maybe you have to accept something. Maybe you have to accept that the world is too big and complicated and full of problems for one individual to make a difference.'

'Even a top bloke like you,' said Dad.

Limpy didn't know what to say.

Perhaps they were right.

He let them both kiss him and give him a hug and tell him that dinner would be ready as soon as they could round up some more insects to replace the ones Goliath had eaten.

After Mum and Dad left, Limpy sat on his bed.

The familiar smell of the dried swampweed always made him feel safe and cosy. Suddenly he wanted to curl up under his moth-wing blanket and never worry about humans again. Never even think about ways to show them that cane toads had a better side.

He lay down and closed his eyes.

But he could still see the stacks of poor dead sun-dried rellies.

And the tighter he squeezed his eyes shut, the more clearly he could imagine Mum and Dad and Charm and Goliath stacked up with them.

7

As the car sped towards Limpy, he waved at it hopefully.

And a bit fearfully.

After all, it was a car and he was a cane toad and this was the highway.

The car hurtled closer.

Limpy closed his eyes. Then opened them again and told himself to stop being a jelly-wart. He waved even harder, hoping desperately the car would swerve across the highway towards him.

Not for the reason cars usually swerved towards cane toads. Limpy didn't want it to drive over him and leave him squashed and stackable.

He wanted the car to pause at his roadside stall so the humans could enjoy some of the snacks and cool drinks he'd prepared for them.

The car didn't swerve or pause.

It hurtled past.

Limpy sighed.

Yet another lot of humans who had no idea how kind and generous cane toads could be.

This wasn't going well. The sun was hot. The grass verge was dry. Every time a vehicle sped past, Limpy got more covered in dust.

'I'll tell you what you need,' said a voice.

Limpy peered around.

A familiar-looking goanna was perched on a branch, nodding at him thoughtfully.

'You need an ad in the local paper,' said the goanna. 'Catering and refreshments section, to let people know what services you're offering. Just tossing it in for what it's worth.'

Limpy was tempted to tell the goanna to mind its own business, but he didn't. He was trying to stay in a kind and generous mood for when the next car came along.

'Mind your own business,' snapped another voice.

Charm hopped out of the undergrowth, glaring at the goanna.

'Suit yourself,' said the goanna, slithering down the tree and waddling off, muttering.

Charm gave Limpy a weary look.

'Local paper, stack me,' she said. 'How in this day and age can a goanna not know about social media?'

Limpy nodded.

He knew how important social media was to humans. You could tell by the way they gawked at it on their phones while they walked into mud holes.

Limpy was hoping human visitors would put his roadside stall onto social media. So other humans would look at it. Instead of at the not very nice phone movie the angry human female had made of Goliath being selfish about Penny in the grotto.

'What are you doing, Limpy?' said Charm, frowning at the roadside stall, which Limpy had to admit was more of a rock.

Limpy explained about the urgent need to show humans that cane toads weren't mean nasty greedy selfish monsters.

'Cool drinks,' he said, pointing to the car hubcap he'd borrowed from Dad's collection. 'I found this left-over hail in a mud hole. As the ice melts, it makes a lovely cool slushy.'

Charm didn't look that impressed.

Limpy saw that the ice had all melted, and in the hot sun the drink didn't look that cool any more, just a bit muddy.

'Snacks,' he said, pointing to the little piles of deliciousness sitting on the swamp leaves arranged attractively around the hubcap. 'I've changed some of Mum's recipes to suit human tastes. See, stuffed wood lice, but I've taken the legs off because they can get stuck between your teeth. Swamp Maggot Delight, but without the pond-scum sauce. Sundried stink bug nibbles, the low-fat ones.'

Charm sighed.

'Do you think I've made the servings too big?' said Limpy. 'I was trying to find a balance between feeding hungry humans and showing them we understand about sensible portion sizes.'

'You never give up, do you, Limpy,' said Charm softly.

Limpy looked at her, puzzled.

He wasn't sure why she'd said that. Of course he didn't give up. When he was very little and the truck had squashed part of his leg, he could have given up then and spent the rest of his life hopping round in circles. But he didn't. He exercised and practised and now he could hop in a completely straight line. Most of the time.

'You've been out here for ages,' said Charm. 'How many cars have stopped?'

Limpy felt an urgent need to tidy the stuffed wood lice.

'Not many,' he mumbled. 'Well, a bit less than that really. None.'

Charm didn't seem surprised.

Limpy decided to ask for her help. She was smart and determined and had great ideas. He was sure she'd be able to think of a way to get cars to stop.

'Charm,' he said. 'Can you help me?'

She sighed and put her head against his chest and hugged him tight.

Limpy felt even more hopeful than when the last car had been hurtling towards him.

But Charm took a step back and looked up at him with a fierce expression.

'I love you, Limpy,' she said. 'So I'll always be

honest with you. This roadside stall plan hasn't got a hope. You'll get sunstroke for starters, and if a vehicle hits you, you'll get multiple fractures and multiple leakages with your insides spurting out.'

Limpy didn't know what to say. Charm was usually a bit more supportive than this.

'So you won't help me?' he said.

Charm shook her head sadly.

'You know I've always helped you in every way I can,' she said. 'But this time, Limpy, only a complete idiot would help you.'

Before Limpy had time to tell her how that made him feel, which was a little bit hurt, there was an explosion of creeper-snapping and cursing in the nearby undergrowth.

Goliath appeared.

'There you are,' he said to Limpy grumpily. 'You can be a really hard bloke to find sometimes. I've been looking everywhere for you.'

'Why?' said Limpy.

He'd been feeling guilty all day about leaving poor heart-broken Goliath alone with his grief.

'Why do you think?' said Goliath, even more grumpily. 'I've come to help.'

8

'This helping caper isn't my idea,' said Goliath, after Charm had given them both long-suffering looks and had gone.

'Whose idea is it?' said Limpy.

'Ancient Abigail's,' said Goliath. 'I asked her if she had any cures for heart-ache and she told me about something that worked for her. But then she said that eating lizard burgers would give me a tummy-ache, so she told me to try something else.'

Goliath burped.

Limpy saw he'd already gobbled three of the snacks.

'Ancient Abigail told you to come here and eat everything on my roadside stall?' said Limpy.

Goliath shook his head.

'I'm just a bit peckish,' he said. 'Ancient Abigail came up with something almost as good, though. She reckons a sure-fire way to forget your own woes is to help others in desperate need.'

Limpy thought about this.

It did sound quite wise.

'Sorry,' he said to Goliath. 'I was a bit ungrateful just then. Actually I could do with some help. I am in a bit of desperate need.'

'Too right you are,' said Goliath, sitting down. 'You're in desperate need for somebody to tell you that this whole roadside stall idea is dopey and stupid, so here I am.'

Goliath popped another two snacks into his mouth.

Limpy stared at him indignantly.

It was bad enough Charm being so hurtful, without Goliath and Ancient Abigail joining in.

'Righty-o,' said Goliath. 'My work here is done. Gee, helping others really gives you an appetite. Have you got any more of these snacks?'

He reached for the last three.

'Hang on,' said Limpy, pushing Goliath's big fist away. 'How can you say this idea's dopey when you haven't even seen if it's working or not?'

With difficulty, Goliath tore his eyes away from the snacks and had a think.

'You've been here most of the day, right?' he said to Limpy. 'How many cars have stopped?'

Limpy decided he didn't want to get into that conversation again.

'If you're really here to lend a hand,' he said to Goliath, 'help me give it one more go. Help me attract the attention of the next humans to drive past.

And if they ignore us, I'll shut the stall down.'

'And I can finish off the snacks?' said Goliath.

Limpy nodded.

'Deal,' said Goliath.

There were no sounds of any approaching vehicles, so Limpy decided to take the weight off his warts for a few moments. He sat down next to Goliath.

As he did, Goliath stood up.

'Don't you think you'd better be on your feet for this lot?' he said.

Limpy peered in the direction Goliath was pointing.

And jumped up.

It was one of the most amazing things he'd ever seen, including lumps of ice raining down in the tropics.

Whizzing towards them along the highway, almost silent except for a faint hiss, was a swarm of giant insects. The ones with their brains on the outside of their heads. The sun was glinting off their shiny multi-coloured bodies and also off their brains.

'Stack me,' breathed Limpy.

Were these the giant relatives of all the insects he and Goliath and the others had ever eaten? Come for terrible revenge?

Limpy was trembling so much he could hardly speak.

'Quick,' he croaked to Goliath. 'Hop for it.'

Goliath hopped for it.

But not, Limpy was horrified to see, away from the advancing giant insects. Towards them.

Limpy went after Goliath to drag him back to safety and to his senses.

Too late.

Goliath was jumping up and down on the edge of the highway, waving his arms and yelling at the giant insects.

'Over here,' he was shouting. 'Free refreshments. The snacks are all reserved, but lovely cool drinks, free of charge.'

The giant insects were very close now.

Limpy made one last desperate attempt to drag Goliath into the undergrowth.

It was no good.

Then Limpy stopped and stared.

The advancing horde weren't insects after all.

They were humans. Humans whose bodies were covered in very tight brightly coloured clothes. Humans who were sitting on thin two-wheeled vehicles, legs moving in a blur.

Limpy recognised the faintly hissing vehicles from tales that older cane toads sometimes told to youngsters. Warning them to keep their hearing alert by not storing snacks in their ears.

Bikes, they were called.

Silent death, the old folk called them.

Just as the old folk had described, the faces of the bike humans were rigid and grim, staring at the highway ahead, not seeing anything around them, including Goliath and Limpy.

'Over here, poo brains,' Goliath was yelling at them. 'Cane toads here who want to show you how kind and generous and friendly we can be. Get your fat bums over here.'

As the first few bike humans whizzed past, they didn't even give Goliath a glance.

Limpy stared at them, disappointed but not surprised.

Balancing on wheels that thin, he thought to himself, must take all your concentration not to fall off, specially with the sun beating down on your naked brains like that.

'You selfish mongrels,' Goliath was yelling. 'You're breaking the heart of a kind sensitive cane toad who wishes you nothing but goodwill, you big lumps of poo. And my cousin feels the same.'

Limpy tried to tell Goliath that it didn't matter, these probably weren't the best humans to be making friends with. But Goliath grabbed a hefty stick lying by the side of the highway.

'Don't worry, Limpy,' he said. 'I'll slow the mongrels down.'

He hurled himself at the last of the bikes as it sped past, and jammed the stick into its back wheel.

And disappeared.

Limpy gasped.

For a moment he thought Goliath had been chewed up by the bike vehicle and spat out in lumps and warts. But then he realised the big spinning blur he could see was Goliath hanging on to the stick wedged in the back wheel.

'Goliath,' he yelled. 'Let go.'

As the bike sped away down the highway, Limpy hopped after it, hoping desperately that Goliath was better at letting go now than he had been with Penny.

His hopes were rewarded.

In the distance two objects flew off the rear wheel of the last bike. Both spun through the air. One was thinner, and Limpy guessed that was the stick. The other was more muscly, and wailing, and Limpy was fairly certain that was Goliath.

Limpy took a while to reach where Goliath landed. It wasn't so much the hopping round in circles problem, it was more the breathing problem he had as he got closer and saw that Goliath wasn't moving.

9

Goliath finally moved.

Just his mouth.

'Penny,' he croaked, his eyes closed.

Limpy felt weak with relief. And concern.

Goliath was alive but he didn't look too good. He'd landed on a flat dusty patch of dirt near the highway. Not much dust, very hard dirt.

'Goliath,' said Limpy, gently touching Goliath's arm. 'Apart from your heart, does anything else feel broken?'

Goliath just groaned, eyes still closed.

Limpy wished he knew more about first aid. The limit of his medical experience was putting aphid ointment on sore warts and helping clear a blocked gullet the time Goliath swallowed a live snake that turned stubborn.

'Doesn't look good,' said a voice.

A group of ants were standing nearby, looking at Goliath and shaking their heads.

'His dribble's gone frothy,' said one. 'That's never a good sign.'

Frothy dribble was leaking out of the corners of Goliath's mouth and dripping off his chin.

Limpy tried to stay calm.

He hoped the ant didn't know much about first aid either and was wrong about frothy dribble being a bad sign. He hoped frothy dribble was just something everyone got when they were spun round very fast on a bike wheel.

Limpy grabbed a leaf and started to wipe the dribble off Goliath's chin. It wasn't exactly first aid, and he wasn't sure if it was helping, but it was all he could think of.

Goliath groaned again, less painfully this time.

'Penny,' he croaked.

He raised one hand, which Limpy hoped was a good sign.

Then he grabbed Limpy's shoulder, which Limpy also hoped was a good sign. But when Goliath clutched at Limpy's other shoulder, and then his chest, Limpy started to have doubts.

'Zip,' mumbled Goliath. 'Where's the zip?'

He opened his eyes and sat up, staring at Limpy in dazed surprise.

'Limpy,' he said. 'I thought you were Penny. I'm hungry. I couldn't find your zip.'

Limpy sagged with relief. If Goliath still had his appetite, he couldn't be too damaged.

'Yum,' exclaimed a voice.

Limpy looked down.

One of the ants was on Goliath's chest, eating some of the frothy dribble.

'This is delicious,' the ant yelled to his friends.

Other ants raced up onto Goliath's chest and soon they were gobbling the frothy dribble too, and agreeing loudly how delicious it was.

'Brush them off,' said Limpy to Goliath. 'They might bite.'

Goliath just sat there, looking at the ants. Limpy started to worry that Goliath might have landed on his head.

All around, ants were rushing out of holes in the ground and hurling themselves onto every puddle and globule of Goliath's dribble they could find.

'Yum,' exclaimed hundreds of voices.

Limpy looked around for something to knock the pesky ants off with. The big green stick that Goliath had jammed into the bike wheel was lying nearby, but it had frothy dribble and gobbling ants on it too.

Limpy grabbed another leaf and turned back to Goliath, who was still just sitting there, staring at the ants on his chest.

This isn't good, thought Limpy. Goliath looks like he's suffering from concussion. And possibly a great big bruise on the brain as well.

He started scraping the ants off Goliath.

'Don't,' said Goliath, pushing the leaf away. 'Leave them.'

Limpy frowned. This wasn't like Goliath at all.

Goliath gently picked up one of the ants from his chest and held it close to his face, peering at it.

'Please,' squeaked the ant. 'Let me have some more. It's the most delicious dessert I've ever tasted. Better than bacteria jelly, better than termite tart, better than anything in the world. Please let me have some more Toad Delight.'

Goliath gently put the ant back onto the frothy dribble.

Amazing, thought Limpy.

He'd never heard of this before. Somebody being made more kind and less greedy by hurtling through the air and landing on their head. Plus, almost as amazingly, Goliath being spun around very fast seemed to have had a delicious effect on his dribble.

Limpy scooped up a bit of frothy dribble from the stick, shook the ants off and cautiously tasted it.

Mmmm, it was delicious. Sweet and tangy and full of yummy flavours.

'Any more ants on the way?' said Goliath.

Limpy looked around at the ant holes. No more ants were hurrying out for Toad Delight.

'Can't see any,' he said.

'Good,' said Goliath. 'Time for tea.'

With both hands, Goliath scooped all the ants off his chest, stuffed them into his mouth and chewed happily.

'Only fair,' he said to Limpy, his cheeks bulging. 'They've had their snack, now I'm having mine.'

Limpy sighed. So much for a blow to the head making someone less greedy. Oh well, at least Goliath was back to his old cheerful self.

Except, Limpy discovered, Goliath didn't stay that way for long. His face crumpled into sadness even while he was still chewing.

'Ancient Abigail was wrong,' wailed Goliath. 'I've been helping you for ages and I haven't forgotten a single woe. I want Penny.'

Limpy's warts twinged with sympathy. He'd never been in love himself, but if it was anything like the times he'd been away from Mum and Dad and Charm, he could guess how much poor Goliath was suffering.

'Try not to think about her,' he said to Goliath. 'Try and enjoy your ants.'

'I can't help it,' said Goliath. 'If an ant feast doesn't stop me thinking about Penny, nothing will.'

He stood up, a bit unsteadily.

'I've got to go and find her,' he said.

Limpy stood up too, alarmed. The whack on Goliath's brain must have made him momentarily forget that Penny's owners had driven off with her ages ago and she could be anywhere in Australia.

In the distance a vehicle was approaching along the highway.

Two vehicles, in fact.

Goliath grabbed the big green stick he'd used before, sucked the last ants off it and hopped wonkily over to the edge of the highway.

He waved the stick at the oncoming vehicles.

Limpy went over to drag him back.

Poor Goliath. He was so brain-scrambled he'd already forgotten about looking for Penny and had gone back to traffic-threatening.

'Over here, big bums,' Goliath yelled at the vehicles. 'Cane toad over here needs a lift to the city.'

Now Limpy understood.

He also understood how unlikely it was that humans would give a cane toad a lift. A whack with a cricket bat, more likely.

He grabbed Goliath, trying to get him away before the humans saw him.

'Don't,' Goliath yelled at Limpy. 'Don't try and stop me. I'm having feelings I've never had before. I know everyone thinks I'm just a big dopey lump. Well, something's changed. I've changed. Love has changed me.'

Limpy let go of Goliath.

He could see on his cousin's face that Goliath meant every croak. And he knew it was coming from Goliath's true heart, not from his greedy tummy or his bruised brain.

The vehicles, both four-wheel drives, were very close now. And slowing down. And stopping.

The humans inside were staring at Goliath.

Limpy hesitated, then ducked into the long grass.

Sometimes, he thought sadly, a toad has to do what a toad has to do. And cop whatever happens.

52

How many times had he said that to Mum and Dad and Charm? About himself.

Limpy watched anxiously as Goliath threw the stick away and jumped onto the back bumper of a four-wheel drive and clung onto the tow bar.

'Thanks,' yelled Goliath. 'Anywhere in the city's fine.'

Limpy waited for a human to get out of the vehicle, pick up the green stick and remove Goliath from the tow bar with it, painfully.

It didn't happen.

Amazingly, the four-wheel drives moved off again.

But not along the highway towards the city.

Limpy watched with growing horror as both the vehicles turned onto a small dirt track and drove slowly along it, away from the highway.

Towards the swamp.

10

Limpy hurried along the dirt track, following the tyre tracks of the four-wheel drives.

As he hopped, he listened anxiously for the sound of cricket bats and tree branches.

The thud of them whacking into Goliath.

Even worse, the sound of them flattening Mum and Dad and Charm as well.

So far, thank swamp, nothing.

All Limpy could hear were his own skin pores gasping for air and, from high above, the voices of a few helpful galahs telling him that the four-wheel drives were parked a little way ahead and were white and had four wheels.

Limpy waved them a thank you.

The track went down into a dip. As Limpy hopped up the other side, he heard sounds nearby.

Not cane toads being hurt. Cane toads having a good time. Laughing and chatting and sometimes even cheering.

Limpy was surprised, but very relieved.

He peeped over the edge of the dip and was even more surprised.

The four-wheel drives were parked at the edge of a clearing in the swamp. Several humans were in the clearing, holding pieces of equipment. All around were cane toads, watching the humans.

Which was OK because the humans weren't doing a single angry or violent thing. Most of them had their backs to the cane toads and were gathered around a picnic table in the middle of the clearing.

Limpy saw what the humans were looking at.

A familiar figure, a large and muscly one, was standing on the table.

Limpy stared.

Goliath seemed to be having a great time. He was grinning and flexing his muscles at the humans, and sometimes turning round and letting them see the tricks he could do with his bottom.

Limpy was amazed. Partly because the humans were all grinning as if they'd never seen anyone pick up twigs between his buttocks before. And partly because Goliath seemed to have forgotten all about his broken heart.

The pieces of equipment, Limpy realised, were cameras and lights and other filming stuff.

The humans were tourists, filming Goliath. Very rich tourists, from the size of their cameras.

Good on you, Goliath, thought Limpy. Good thinking, taking your mind off your broken heart by spending time on one of your favourite hobbies.

Showing off.

The humans were enjoying it too. They really liked Goliath, Limpy could see. With a bit of luck, when they got back home they'd show their holiday videos to all their friends. And when people saw that Goliath wasn't stuffing a single thing into his mouth, word would spread that cane toads weren't greedy after all, just friendly.

Limpy hopped closer for a better look.

At the edge of the clearing he felt something hard under his foot. He stopped, but before he could see what it was, he felt something else.

Hot breath on his back.

Limpy turned.

All he saw at first were big teeth and fierce eyes.

He hopped back, poison glands ready to squirt in self-defence. Then he saw who the teeth and eyes belonged to.

A dog.

Limpy recognised the dog's breed. Tourists had brought dogs like this into the swamp before. A parrot had told him humans called this breed Blue Heeler. Which Limpy thought was a dopey name as the dog clearly didn't have blue heels. Perhaps it meant the dog liked to eat things with blue heels.

The dog was glaring at Limpy.

Limpy was glad his heels were greeny-brown and warty rather than blue.

'Step off the cable,' said the dog.

Limpy wasn't sure what the dog meant. Then he remembered the thing under his feet. He looked down. He was standing on an electrical cable, just like the ones humans used to connect their hairdryers to their campervans, only thicker.

'Here's my suggestion,' said the dog. 'If you step off the cable, I won't have to hurt you and you won't want to hurt me back and we'll all be completely unhurt, you, me and the cable.'

Limpy hopped off the cable.

'Good man,' said the dog. 'Thank you.'

'You're welcome,' said Limpy.

'Nice place you've got here,' said the dog.

'Thanks,' said Limpy.

He was about to say goodbye and go over to Goliath, but he stopped. The dog seemed friendly and only a little bit violent. Goliath was doing such a good job with the humans, Limpy decided he might as well stay and chat. Dogs knew a lot of humans. Maybe this one would help spread the message about friendly cane toads.

'Have you been to a swamp before?' Limpy asked.

'Heaps,' said the dog. 'We shoot in them a lot.'

Limpy went tense until he remembered that 'shoot' was another word for 'film'.

'We're a TV crew from the city,' said the dog. 'My human takes care of the cameras and things.'

Limpy's insides gave a little hop of excitement.

'Are you making a TV show about cane toads?' he asked.

The dog hesitated.

'Sort of,' it replied.

Limpy pointed to the picnic table, where Goliath was entertaining another human, a woman with elegant black hair and red lips and a friendly face. She was tickling Goliath's tummy and feeding him grasshoppers.

'Will Goliath be on TV?' asked Limpy.

The dog hesitated again.

'Sort of,' it said.

Limpy was puzzled. For someone who'd started a conversation, the dog wasn't a very good converser.

'Anyway,' said the dog, 'can't stand here chatting. We'll be packing up soon. Nice to meet you.'

Limpy said it was nice for him too, then hopped closer to the picnic table, hoping to catch Goliath's eye and signal to him to slow down with the grasshopper eating and perhaps offer them around to the humans.

Before he could, Charm came over, breathless with what Limpy assumed was excitement.

'Look,' she said, pointing to the picnic table.

'I know,' said Limpy. 'Isn't it fantastic? Goliath's going to be on a TV show about cane toads, and as far as I can tell it's a show about how funny and friendly and clever with our buttocks we are.'

Limpy wanted to say, 'and also how we're not the slightest bit greedy,' but he was starting to get worried by how many grasshoppers Goliath was eating.

'No,' said Charm, 'it isn't fantastic at all.'

She wasn't just breathless, Limpy realised, she was also upset, and pointing urgently at the table.

Limpy saw why.

Goliath was really showing off now, stuffing lots of grasshoppers into his mouth, and a couple of pens, and the TV woman's makeup bag.

The TV woman didn't seem upset. She was laughing. And offering Goliath one of her shoes.

An awful thought burned through Limpy.

What if this isn't a nice TV show about how friendly and funny and kind and generous cane toads are? What if it's like the horrible one on Ancient Abigail's tablet about how we're mean and greedy and in urgent need of being stamped out?

That would explain why the TV woman was trying to make Goliath look as greedy as possible by giving him her other shoe.

All Goliath cares about, thought Limpy gloomily, is getting a lift to the city to find Penny, so no wonder he's going along with it. Specially as he likes eating shoes so much.

'Look,' said Charm again with an anguished croak.

Limpy saw that Charm wasn't pointing at Goliath, she was pointing under the table.

Goliath's energetic gobbling was making the table shake. Under the table, a cloth cover was sliding off something.

Limpy's warts froze with horror.

It was a wire cage, full of cane toads, all struggling to get out.

'Goliath,' yelled Limpy, partly as a warning and partly to let Goliath know an urgent rescue was needed.

But Goliath was so deeply involved with showing off, he hadn't even noticed the cage.

The other cane toads had.

Screams and croaks rang through the clearing.

Rellies and neighbours hopped in every direction.

Limpy heard a familiar wail from the table.

Goliath, he saw, had finally noticed the cage full of cane toads. Mostly because the TV woman had picked him up and put him in with them.

Limpy flung himself towards the cage.

The clearing was in complete chaos. Cane toads were desperately trying to get out of the way of one of the four-wheel drives. It was revving its engine, and the TV woman and several of the other humans were getting in.

Limpy tried to struggle through the crowd.

He couldn't.

Too late.

Another human opened the back flap of the four-wheel drive and put the cage of cane toads inside and closed the flap.

The four-wheel drive accelerated away.

Limpy felt someone grab him. It was Charm.

'They're taking Goliath,' she said. 'We have to do something.'

'One of us has to keep Mum and Dad safe,' said Limpy. 'We can't leave them alone. I'll get Goliath back.'

Charm looked at Limpy, and he could see from the fierce gleam in her eyes that she thought she'd be better at getting Goliath back.

Limpy gave her a pleading look.

One that said, I have to do this. Because if I hadn't been so dopey with all that stuff about a toad doing what a toad's got to do, Goliath wouldn't be in a cage in a TV vehicle heading to who-knows-where.

'Let me do it,' he said to Charm. 'Please.'

Charm gave him another look, still fierce but also understanding.

She hugged him and went.

Limpy squinted down the bush track. The four-wheel drive was already out of sight.

But the other one wasn't.

It was still parked.

Limpy headed towards it.

11

'A lift?'

The Blue Heeler frowned at Limpy and showed even more of its teeth.

Limpy had the feeling this dog wasn't a big lift-giver. It was hard to imagine this dog ever grinning and saying 'hop in', not even if Limpy's heels were bright blue with attractive turquoise stripes.

'Please,' begged Limpy.

'Begging isn't very dignified,' said the dog.

'I'm doing it for my cousin,' said Limpy. 'He's in the other four-wheel drive. I need to rescue him.'

The dog looked uncomfortable and rubbed its back against a tyre.

Limpy wasn't sure if the dog had fleas or was just worried by the thought of how dangerous the rescue would be.

'I need to go where the other four-wheel drive has gone, said Limpy. 'I'm only asking for a lift. I'm not asking you to do the actual rescue.'

The dog was still looking uncomfortable.

'You don't want to go to that place,' it said. 'You don't want to see what's going to happen there.'

'What do you mean?' said Limpy.

'You don't want to know,' said the dog.

Limpy took a deep breath.

Goliath needed him to be patient now. No yelling or squirting poison or trying to get one of the dog's feet into his mouth.

Limpy wondered if he could stow away on the four-wheel drive without the dog knowing. Probably not. The dog's job was obviously to guard things. With its teeth.

'Anyway,' said the dog. 'What makes you think you can even rescue your cousin? One of the biggest TV networks in the country needs him for more filming back in the studio. Which has security like you wouldn't believe. Have you seen the movie *Escape From Alcatraz*?'

'No,' said Limpy.

'Nor have I,' said the dog. 'I tried to sneak in to see it, but studio security wouldn't let me. They are so tough.'

Limpy lost his patience.

'I know how to rescue my own cousin, alright?' he snapped at the dog.

'How?' growled the dog.

Limpy hesitated. He may have exaggerated a bit about the actual knowing. But he was sure he could come up with something.

'In my family,' said Limpy quietly, 'we believe one individual can make a difference.'

The dog opened its mouth to say something scornful, then closed it again and stared at Limpy, impressed.

'That is a great concept,' said the dog. 'That would make a great TV show. I should pitch that idea to the network. A show about small, slightly squashed individuals who make a difference. That's exactly what I've been looking for to get my TV career off the ground. With an idea like that they'd make me an associate producer, minimum.'

'Give me a lift,' said Limpy, 'and it's yours.'

'Deal,' said the dog. 'I'll get back to you as soon as I can. Sometimes my human takes a little while to get what I'm telling him, but you'll have that lift in two weeks, three tops.'

Limpy gave an anguished croak.

'I need the lift now,' he said.

The dog wasn't even listening. It was gazing into the distance, obviously dreaming about the kind of office or kennel an associate producer would have.

Limpy didn't have time to wait.

He hopped away from the four-wheel drive, careful to avoid the remaining humans who were packing up their gear.

At least he knew where Goliath was being taken.

I'll get to the city somehow, thought Limpy. I'll hitchhike or borrow a skateboard or swim through sewer pipes or something.

His leg gave a twitch. A storm was coming.

And along with it, an idea.

Limpy hopped back to the four-wheel drive.

'Here's an even better idea,' he said to the dog. 'With this one they'll make you a primary producer.'

Limpy explained about his crook leg and how it knew when a storm was on the way. Then he pointed to the hail dents in the four-wheel drive.

'Seems to me,' he said, 'humans need a bit of help with their weather predicting. Which I can give them, live on TV. The world's first weather toad.'

Limpy held his breath.

The dog's eyes were shining.

'Brilliant,' it said.

'One condition,' said Limpy. 'I get the lift now.'

The dog hesitated, looking at Limpy and frowning.

'How do I know you're telling the truth?' it said. 'Not just pitching me a yarn?'

'Simple,' said Limpy. 'See how blue the sky is and how there's not a whisper of a breeze? Give it a few minutes.'

They did.

The storm hit suddenly and violently.

As the rain smashed down, the humans threw the last bits of equipment into the four-wheel drive and dived inside themselves.

Limpy huddled in the undergrowth.

The rain was making him shiver, and so were some second thoughts.

Once the humans found out what his leg could do, he'd be kept in the TV weather studio for ever.

He'd never see the swamp again. Or Mum or Dad or Charm. And they'd only ever see him on Ancient Abigail's tablet, if she ever got the battery recharged.

'Hey,' called a voice.

Limpy looked up. In their haste to get out of the rain, the humans had left the rear flap of the four-wheel drive open a crack. A nose was poking out.

'Hop in,' called the dog.

Limpy sighed.

He'd be a prisoner for life.

Freedom gone.

Would the sacrifice be worth it if he could rescue Goliath and the other cane toads in the cage? Plus help keep humans safe from violent storms and as a result keep Mum and Dad and Charm safe from violent humans?

Limpy sighed again.

Of course it would.

12

After the rain stopped smashing onto the roof of the four-wheel drive, the loudest noise on the journey to the city was the thudding of Limpy's heart.

He hoped only he could hear it.

The driver was listening to music and the other humans were dozing. So was the dog, curled up on some cables in the back.

Limpy couldn't sleep.

The camera case he was hiding in also had a camera in it. Cameras, Limpy discovered, were very selfish about sharing space. Plus Limpy had too many thoughts racing through his mind for sleep.

The dog had said Goliath was being taken to the TV studio for more filming, and something was going to happen there that Limpy wouldn't want to know about.

Limpy had a horrible idea what it might be.

If the TV show was about how cane toads were greedy selfish monsters, the producers would almost certainly want a segment called 'How To Kill A Cane Toad'. And they'd want a big greedy-looking one to demonstrate on. To show exactly how to do the bashing. And the stabbing. And the squashing flat.

'Oh, Goliath,' groaned Limpy.

He rolled over to ease his aching back and anxious thoughts. As he did, he bumped the lid of the camera case, which opened a crack.

Quickly he tried to close it.

Yellow light was seeping in.

Even though Limpy was panicking a bit, he couldn't help noticing the light was an unusual colour.

It wasn't the colour of moonlight, and Limpy was pretty sure if humans were checking to see if a cane toad was hiding in their camera case, the torchlight wouldn't just seep in like this. It would pour in after the camera case lid was flung open and then it would flash around a lot while the humans tried to bash the cane toad with the torch.

Curious, Limpy pushed the camera case lid open a bit more and peeked out.

Through the back window of the vehicle he could see the dark sky and lots of yellow moons. Rows of them, floating past, one by one.

They looked strange and beautiful, if a bit small.

That's weird, thought Limpy. At our place I've only ever seen two moons, the one in the sky and the one in the swamp water.

Perhaps it isn't only the weather that's changing.

Perhaps the moons are too.

Then Limpy noticed, between two of the moons, a huge pair of glowing golden buttocks.

He'd seen those buttocks before. They were the golden buttocks on hamburger boxes that humans sometimes threw out of cars.

Hamburger boxes from the city.

Limpy realised these moons weren't moons, they were something he'd heard glow worms whispering about.

City street lights.

Limpy tensed. It was time.

In his mind he ran through the list of things he had to do.

Get away from the dog and the humans. Rescue Goliath and the other cane toads. Find the TV managers and demonstrate his storm-alert leg and become the network weather toad so that every time humans turned on a screen to check the weather they'd be reminded how friendly and generous and useful cane toads could be.

It seemed a lot.

Limpy didn't panic. He remembered the advice Dad gave him when they were taking the rude bits off centipedes so Mum could stuff slugs with them.

That had been a lot to think about too, but Dad had made it easier.

'Don't try and do it all at once,' he'd said to Limpy. 'One thing at a time.'

Limpy knew the first thing he had to do now.

Be patient and stay hidden until they got to the TV studio.

He managed it. And he knew when they'd finally arrived because the huge building they stopped in front of had a familiar sign on the wall, the same sign that was on the side of the four-wheel drive.

A big gate slid open and a human in a uniform waved them through.

Limpy took some deep breaths.

This next bit wasn't going to be easy, even doing one thing at a time.

As soon as the four-wheel drive was parked, Limpy hopped out of the camera case.

The dog was waking up, yawning and stretching.

'We're here,' said the dog to Limpy. 'Time for me to introduce you to my human. Don't worry, he won't hurt you once he realises we've got an idea for a TV series.'

Limpy didn't reply.

He stayed in the shadows until the humans got out of the four-wheel drive and opened the back flap. He waited until one of them picked up a heavy camera case.

Then he flung himself up onto the case and did a loud croak right into the human's face and poked his tongue out.

The human, startled, dropped the case.

Limpy bounced off the case and rolled painfully across the ground.

He didn't mind.

As he'd hoped, the humans were yelling and fumbling with the case, trying to see if the camera was broken.

Limpy hopped across the dark carpark in a fairly straight line to a pile of rubbish. He squirted the pile with his poison glands, then headed on to some bushes at the edge of the carpark.

'Come back,' he heard the dog calling. 'Weather toad. Where are you?'

Limpy crouched under the bushes.

After a while, he saw the dog sniffing around the pile of rubbish. The dog stayed sniffing a long time, sure from the smell that Limpy was in there. But eventually a human whistled and the dog gave up.

'We had a deal,' howled the dog into the night. 'You selfish greedy wartbag.'

Limpy tried not to feel guilty.

He waited until the lights in the building went out and the humans got into their own cars, one of them with the dog, and drove out through the gate.

He waited while the guard locked the door of the little room next to the gate and walked off down the street.

Then he went to rescue Goliath.

The first four-wheel drive, the one Goliath had been taken away in, was standing in the carpark.

Limpy hopped over to it.

'Goliath,' he called.

No reply.

Limpy dragged himself up onto the roof of the

71

four-wheel drive and hopped around as noisily as he could. Goliath was a heavy sleeper but he couldn't bear anything jumping around near his head, which is why he always checked his scalp for fleas and frogs before he went to sleep.

Nothing.

Goliath wasn't in there.

Must be in the building, thought Limpy. They mustn't have wanted him peeing in the vehicle.

Limpy went over to the main building and quickly discovered that the dog had been right about the security.

Everything was locked, shuttered, bolted and screwed down tight.

The big roller doors sat in specially made grooves in the ground so not even an ant who wanted to audition for a gardening show could get in.

The windows all had rubber seals, the air-conditioning ducts on the roof were all welded shut and the stormwater pipes all had mesh drain covers on them.

Limpy tried desperately to shift the mesh.

He couldn't. He dragged himself wearily away from the last pipe.

Who would put drain covers on a drain? he thought bitterly. A TV studio who doesn't want a cane toad to be rescued, that's who.

Limpy sighed. He'd have to wait till morning.

He hoped the studio didn't do filming at night. Specially not a segment with Goliath in it called

'How To Kill A Cane Toad'. He hoped they were going to wait till morning as well.

They probably will, Limpy told himself. They probably want whoever does the killing to be well rested and not drop the cricket bat or the tree branch on anyone's foot.

First thing tomorrow, Limpy promised himself, as soon as they open up, I'll get in there and find Goliath.

He went back to the corner of the carpark and flopped down under the bushes. He tried to go to sleep, but couldn't stop thinking about things.

Mostly how he'd scared a human on purpose and let a dog down when they had a deal.

This is dopey, thought Limpy. I'm trying to show humans how kind and generous and friendly cane toads can be, and instead I've been mean and nasty and selfish.

He hoped the humans never found out, or the weather, or either of the moons.

13

The early-morning sun twinkled painfully through Limpy's eyelids.

He tried to ignore it.

Couldn't the sun see this wasn't the time for painful twinkling? Didn't it know a cane toad who needed more sleep when it saw one?

Clearly not.

Then Limpy realised the sun was doing him a favour. It was giving him a hint. How To Rescue A Cane Toad, Lesson One.

Start early.

Limpy opened his eyes and dragged himself to his feet.

Ow.

TV studio carparks were very stiff and sore places to sleep. Gritty and lumpy and not the slightest bit nice and swampy. But that wasn't the sun's fault.

'Thank you, sun,' said Limpy.

He peered at the TV studio building, hoping to

see a door or a window or a drain cover that had been opened to greet the new morning.

Nothing. All still shut.

Limpy remembered Dad's advice and tried not to see the locked-down roller door as a disastrous barrier to Goliath's survival.

He tried to see it as a centipede's rude bit.

One thing at a time.

Limpy hopped towards the other side of the building to see if anything was open there. He was hopeful. Lots of cars were in the carpark, so the TV studio workers must already have arrived.

Human voices were chattering in the distance.

Limpy didn't want to run into any humans, just the doors or windows he hoped they'd left open. With, he hoped, no guards on duty to stamp out rescue attempts.

He reached the other side of the building.

And froze.

Oh no.

Word must have spread he was on the premises.

Hundreds of guards were standing in a long line, almost the whole length of the building.

Luckily the guards hadn't seen him. And at least they didn't look ruthless or violent. Most of them weren't even wearing uniforms. Just, Limpy was puzzled to see, t-shirts with pictures of cane toads on them.

It must be so they can identify what they're guarding against, he thought.

Slowly Limpy started to edge away.

Then he stopped, even more puzzled.

Some of the guards were holding fluffy toys.

Not just any fluffy toys. Fluffy cane toad toys. Which might also have been to help identify the enemy. Except the guards were cuddling the toys as if they liked them.

Other guards with big plastic sacks were handing out more t-shirts and cane toad toys to guards who didn't have them.

What was going on?

Limpy couldn't resist hopping a little closer to get a better look. He quickly wished he hadn't.

Human hands grabbed him and before he could say 'put me down, I'm warty,' he was up in the air, surrounded by human faces staring at him.

But not staring angrily. Not even sternly. Most of the faces were smiling and laughing, as if they were pleased to see him.

Limpy didn't understand.

He peered out from the two cupped human hands he was nestled in, trying to make sense of the long row of human guards with their cane toad toys and cane toad t-shirts. Some of them were even holding posters that had cane toads on them surrounded by love hearts.

Limpy had a crazy thought.

These humans didn't look like guards at all. They looked more like fans.

Cane toad fans.

As Limpy trembled at the amazingness of that possibility, the humans suddenly gave a cheer.

For a giddy moment Limpy thought they were cheering him. But they weren't. A big roller door was opening and a couple of real guards, with uniforms and everything, were beckoning the queue of humans to come inside.

Limpy huddled down into the cupped hands. He let himself be carried along in the crowd of chattering humans, grateful for the lift. The thoughts he was having were making him feel so excited he could hardly breathe.

If these humans were fans, they were probably here to watch the TV show being made. And cane toad fans would not come to watch a show about cane toad badness.

Cane toad niceness, more like.

Limpy was so excited, he almost wet himself.

Then he did wet himself. It was the quickest way to make the human drop him so he could have a squiz inside the studio and find out if he was right about the show.

Amazing. The human dropped him but didn't get angry, not even with toad pee on his hands. He just laughed and wiped his hands on a friend.

Limpy hopped away.

The TV studio was amazing too.

It was lit as brightly as a campground shower block, but a million times bigger. On one side were rows of seats on steps, like in a country town cricket ground. All over the floor were cables, but not, Limpy was relieved to see, any dogs.

And in a corner was a wire cage with one figure in it, all alone. The figure Limpy most wanted to see in the whole world.

'Goliath,' he croaked.

He hopped towards the cage, ducking between human feet and nearly getting squashed by huge cameras on wheels.

Goliath looked up and his grin stretched across half the cage.

'Limpy,' he said. 'You made it. I knew you would. I knew you'd get here in time to see me be a star.'

Limpy stared at his cousin.

Was Goliath joking, to keep their spirits up?

'These TV production humans love me,' said Goliath. 'They particularly like my cheeks. A dog who understands their language told me. So I assume they like my whole face.'

Limpy felt relief relaxing his own face. If Goliath was right, this was wonderful.

'I'm the star of the show,' said Goliath. 'We did a rehearsal before and it was mostly about me. Specially my body parts.'

Given a choice, Limpy would have preferred to hear Goliath say 'Specially my kind and generous personality', but it was still wonderful.

'Now that I'm a big star,' continued Goliath dreamily, 'Penny will come back to me, I know she will. Her family will be so proud to see us together.

I'll give them autographs or some frothy dribble or something.'

Limpy wasn't sure how proud they'd be, but that could wait till later. For now he had to be sure Goliath was going to be OK.

'What kind of show is this exactly?' he said to Goliath.

'A really good one about me,' said Goliath.

Before Limpy could ask for more details, Goliath pointed to a couple of human production assistants heading their way.

'Looks like we're about to start,' said Goliath. 'I'm not sure exactly how the show works, but take a seat and you'll see for yourself.'

All the seats had humans sitting in them, so Limpy made do with a patch of floor under a rack of clothes near a wall.

A thought hit him.

He wished he'd asked Goliath about the other cane toads who were in the cage. Oh well, he'd probably see them in the show.

Limpy watched a human production assistant lift Goliath out of the cage and carefully carry him to a table with trays of makeup on it. Limpy knew about makeup. Goliath had eaten some in a shower block once.

The production assistant made a chair out of his hands so Goliath could sit comfortably.

A human makeup expert started work. Gently and with great concentration, she brushed and dusted and smoothed makeup onto Goliath's front and back and even under his arms.

Goliath giggled. Limpy wasn't surprised. This was the very first time Goliath had ever had makeup on his outside.

Limpy felt himself grinning.

Goliath really was a star.

Amazing.

And it was excellent that Goliath was so keen to impress Penny's family. Because that meant he probably wouldn't do anything too greedy.

Limpy settled back to enjoy the show. He hadn't felt this happy for . . . he couldn't remember how long. Since he was a little kid on a mud slide probably.

He gazed around and saw that part of the studio was a large kitchen. Must be in case Goliath needed a snack.

The kitchen didn't have any walls.

Limpy guessed why. The production people had probably discovered that when Goliath got hungry, it was urgent. And if there were walls in the way, Goliath tried to go through them.

That's very considerate and generous of the production people, thought Limpy. Very extremely generous. Very remarkably generous in fact.

A faint worry started to niggle at Limpy's warts.

If he forced himself to think honestly about it, it did seem almost unbelievably generous.

'Are you a keen cook too?' said a voice.

A mosquito landed next to Limpy.

'Cook?' said Limpy. 'Why do you ask?'

He wondered if the mosquito had mistaken him for Goliath's personal chef.

'We're all keen cooks here in the cooking show audience,' said the mosquito. 'I'm here to expand my culinary repertoire. Give my family the chance to try new things. They are so unadventurous, my family. All they want for dinner is blood.'

'Did you say cooking show?' said Limpy, a chill gripping his warts.

'That's right,' said the mosquito. 'She's our favourite TV chef. Always cooking weird unusual things. And after she does, they become crazes around the world.'

Limpy started to feel ill.

The mosquito stared at him.

'Oh dear, I'm so sorry,' it said. 'I didn't notice. I thought you were an audience member. But you're more of a, what would you call it, ingredient.'

Limpy hoped he hadn't heard right.

'Did you say ingredient?' he croaked.

The mosquito looked embarrassed.

'Sorry,' it said. 'Not very tactful of me. But I didn't know how else to put it. Because of the main recipe on today's show. The dish she's going to cook for the nation. Cane toad cheeks.'

Limpy stared at the mosquito, horrified.

He looked across at Goliath.

Goliath was in the studio kitchen, which Limpy

81

now realised must be the cooking show set. He was sitting on one end of a kitchen bench, on a chopping board. He gave Limpy a grin and a thumbs up.

Limpy felt sick.

'This is crazy,' said Limpy to the mosquito. 'We cane toads have got poison glands near our cheeks. Any human who eats our cheeks will die.'

The mosquito shook its head.

'Sorry again,' it said. 'Cheeks is cooking lingo. When I say cheeks, I don't mean the ones you're gabbing with, I mean the ones you're sitting on.'

The mosquito pointed to the kitchen bench.

At the other end of the bench from Goliath, a production assistant was putting down a large platter piled with pale, skinless, but familiar objects.

'Those are some she prepared earlier,' said the mosquito.

Limpy stared at the platter, aghast.

He'd never seen them like that before, but he knew exactly what they were.

Cane toad buttocks.

14

The cooking show started.

Limpy huddled under the rack of clothes.

He felt like his brains were being fried. Not because he was anywhere near sizzling olive oil or bubbling butter.

Because of what he was seeing.

The human woman with the black hair and red lips, the one who'd been so friendly to Goliath in the swamp, was standing on the set behind the kitchen bench. She was wearing a white coat now, to show she was the chef. And she wasn't being so friendly to Goliath.

She was holding him upside down in front of a camera and prodding his buttocks with a fork. Goliath was starting to look doubtful. She obviously hadn't used a fork in rehearsals.

Limpy couldn't understand what the woman was saying, but he guessed. She was demonstrating how to choose a yummy pair of cane toad buttocks.

Plumpness is very important, she was probably saying. And tenderness. And juiciness.

Limpy felt sick with panic.

Goliath wasn't looking too happy either. He gave an alarmed croak as he spotted the tray of cane toad buttocks prepared earlier and the big pan of sizzling oil and butter on the stove top.

Limpy knew he had to move fast.

In a few minutes the studio audience would be sampling fried cane toad cheeks, including Goliath's, and across the nation a new food craze would be born.

No cane toad's bottom would be safe ever again. Soon it wouldn't be golden buttocks printed on wrappers and boxes that humans threw out of cars, it would be cane toad buttocks.

Limpy tried to think what to do.

He was pretty sure that leaping onto the set and offering his services as a weather toad probably wasn't going to work. Not with a bottom-prodding chef in charge and a studio audience hungry for fried cane toad delicacies.

He needed to offer something that would satisfy seriously hungry humans. Something that would delight their tastebuds even more than a juicy buttock.

Limpy saw the chef put Goliath into an empty saucepan and keep him there with a heavy lid. She started preparing another part of the recipe, mixing together flour and water.

I know what that is, thought Limpy.

Whenever he'd seen human fried food, it always had batter on it. The chef was planning to make battered buttocks.

Limpy stared at the machine she was using to make the batter. A machine that whizzed everything round, very fast.

And suddenly he knew what he had to do.

Yes, of course.

Limpy hopped across the studio floor and dragged himself up onto the kitchen bench.

Goliath had forced part of his head out from under the saucepan lid.

'Limpy, no,' he croaked. 'Save yourself. I'll choke as many of them as I can with my buttocks. Get away, Limpy.'

Limpy ignored him. There wasn't time to chat, not even with the bravest most generous cousin in the world.

The whizzing machine was still whizzing.

Another sound filled the studio. The sound of applause. Limpy saw that the humans in the studio audience were laughing and clapping.

At him.

This was good. If humans were pleased to see him, they'd probably be happy to have a taste of what he was about to prepare for them.

Toad Delight.

Limpy dived into the whizzing machine.

It was like being hit by a truck. Everything went

blurry and Limpy felt himself being sucked through the sticky batter and splayed against the wall of the metal bowl. He felt his cheeks, both pairs, being dragged in strange directions by the force of the whiz.

Then suddenly everything started to slow down.

Limpy guessed the chef must have turned off the machine.

When the machine stopped, Limpy peered woozily over the edge of the bowl. The whole TV studio was spinning around slowly, and the studio audience were looking a bit stunned, which Limpy assumed was because the TV people hadn't warned them a TV studio could do that.

Limpy saw what he was looking for.

A bowl of sponge-cake pieces near him on the kitchen bench. Prepared earlier, Limpy guessed, for when the chef did the dessert part of the show.

Well, thought Limpy, the dessert part is now.

He scraped his hand across his face to get a big glob of frothy dribble to fling onto the sponge cake and create, for the very first time on national television, Toad Delight.

Except there wasn't any frothy dribble.

Limpy frantically felt his mouth, his chin, his nose, his ears.

Nothing.

He looked desperately over at Goliath, who was struggling to get out from under the saucepan lid.

'Goliath,' he yelled. 'I need you. Over here.'

With a super-amphibian effort, Goliath pushed the lid off the saucepan. It clanged to the studio floor, which made the chef yell angrily at the production assistants before she remembered she was on camera.

'Goliath,' yelled Limpy. 'Quick.'

Goliath was across the kitchen bench in a couple of hops. The second hop brought him thudding onto the START button of the whizzing machine.

'Good on you, Goliath,' croaked Limpy.

As the machine started to spin again, Limpy grabbed Goliath and dragged him into the bowl.

'This won't feel very nice,' he shouted into Goliath's ear. 'But you're doing it for cane toads everywhere.'

The machine didn't spin for long.

Limpy knew it probably wouldn't.

But it was long enough.

As the motor was switched off and the spinning bowl slowed down, Limpy got control of his cheeks and gave a yell of triumph.

Goliath's frothy dribble was everywhere.

All over him and Goliath. And, most importantly, all over the bowl of sponge cake.

'You did it, Goliath,' said Limpy.

'Grrggglllgh,' replied Goliath, and sprayed another stream of frothy dribble into the air.

Limpy waited for the machine and the studio to stop spinning so he could introduce Toad Delight to the human world. He planned to use the big toothy grins humans seemed to like on TV. Plus lots of tasting samples.

Except, as Limpy's vision stopped spinning, he saw that it wasn't only the sponge cake that was drenched in frothy dribble.

The kitchen bench was too, and the chef, and the production assistants, and several cameras, and the front few rows of the studio audience.

Oh no, thought Limpy. This might not be how humans like their dessert.

The humans on the set were staggering around, trying to wipe the frothy dribble out of their eyes. The ones in the studio audience were starting to make a panicked dash for the exits.

Limpy stood waist-deep in batter, helplessly watching them go.

'Come on,' said Goliath, dragging himself out of the bowl. 'Don't just stand here. We've got to get moving. We can lick the batter off as we hop.'

Limpy was impressed by Goliath's clear thinking. Usually when trouble happened, all Goliath wanted to do was find something to hit with a stick.

'You're right,' Limpy said. 'We should hide for a while. Give the humans a chance to calm down and change their minds about Toad Delight.'

He saw that Goliath didn't agree.

Goliath was looking at him as if he was crazy.

'We're not hiding,' said Goliath, pointing towards one of the exits. 'We're chasing.'

Limpy saw what Goliath was pointing at.

On the back of a departing human child was a familiar face. Big dark eyes, shiny black fur, a beautiful yellow beak, plus blue zip-up pockets and red plastic straps.

'Penny,' yelled Goliath. 'Wait for me.'

He hopped off the kitchen bench and lumbered across the studio floor.

'Come back,' yelled Limpy.

Goliath ignored him.

The human child had already disappeared through the exit, and Goliath followed, still calling Penny's name.

Limpy was torn.

If he stayed and persuaded some of the humans to taste the Toad Delight that was still lying around on the set, they might love it.

Love it so much they'd never slaughter another cane toad for its buttocks. Want it so much they'd let cane toads live in peace and dignity, gratefully accepting all the frothy dribble that cane toads generously gave them.

On the other hand, thought Limpy anxiously, there's Goliath.

Humans around the country were probably feeling very cross about the big mess made on their favourite cooking show. Word was probably getting round that toads had done it.

So a cane toad roaming the streets of the city, dopey and lovesick and splattered with batter, could be in serious danger.

And, Limpy feared, it could get even worse.

The human child carrying Penny today looked different to the human child Limpy had seen with Penny in the swamp.

This new child was probably a friend or relative. She wouldn't know who Goliath was or why he wanted her backpack. Neither would her parents. Which could result in even more violence than before.

Mostly to Goliath.

Limpy sighed, dragged himself out of the bowl, hopped onto the studio floor and, as quickly as he could, avoiding cables and angry humans, followed Goliath's trail of batter.

15

Outside the TV studio, Limpy couldn't see Goliath anywhere.

Just his batter, a few blobs of it, in the gutter.

Limpy's warts tingled hopefully. Perhaps there was a trail of batter. Perhaps it would show him which way Goliath had gone.

He found a couple more blobs, but no trail.

The road was jammed with buses and cars full of scowling humans from the studio audience.

From the looks on their faces, and the lumps of dried frothy dribble also on their faces, Limpy could see they weren't cane toad fans any more.

Fluffy cane toad toys had already been squashed flat on the road.

Limpy looked anxiously, but he couldn't see a big muscly real cane toad squashed among them.

Penny was nowhere to be seen either.

I need an eyewitness, thought Limpy. Somebody who saw them and can tell me which way they went.

He noticed that the blobs of Goliath's batter were being nibbled by a couple of flies. He decided to start with them.

As he got closer, he saw a familiar mosquito chatting with the flies.

'Turns out,' the mosquito was saying, 'if you fillet them carefully and pan-fry them in oil and butter, they're quite safe to eat. You'd never guess they come from such rough-looking raw ingredients. Not that we'll ever get the chance to taste them. After what those clowns did in there, no human will touch a cane toad buttock with a barge pole or a recipe book.'

The mosquito saw Limpy and stammered into an awkward silence.

'Excuse me,' said Limpy. 'I was wondering if you could help me.'

'I am so deeply embarrassed,' said the mosquito. 'I shouldn't have been talking like that. But these blokes are cooking fans and they didn't see the show because if they turn up without tickets, they get sprayed.'

'When you say help you,' said one of the flies, 'do you mean eat some of that unsightly batter off your knees?'

The two flies looked hopeful.

Limpy shook his head.

Normally he liked inviting guests to lunch, but today there was no time.

'I was wondering if either of you have seen my

cousin Goliath,' said Limpy. 'He looks a bit like me but with much bigger muscles.'

'And wonderful buttocks,' said the mosquito.

Limpy gave it a look.

'Sorry,' mumbled the mosquito.

'Goliath was chasing after his girlfriend,' said Limpy to the flies. 'Penguin backpack, yellow beak, fully insulated. He's so in love you wouldn't believe it. I'm worried about what will happen to him if he can't find her. She's the only backpack in the world for him.'

The flies looked at each other, and Limpy had the feeling there was something they wanted to tell him but didn't know how.

'Um,' said one of the flies.

The other pointed along the street.

'Go all the way to the end,' it said. 'Then turn left. Bit further on you'll find what it is you're, you know, um . . . looking for.'

'Goliath and Penny?' said Limpy.

'When you say Penny,' said the first fly, 'do you mean the only backpack in the world?'

Limpy nodded.

The flies gave each other another look.

'Just Penny,' said one.

'Sort of,' said the other.

'You'll understand when you get there,' said the first fly.

Limpy wished he understood now.

But Penny was better than nothing.

Wherever Penny was, Limpy hoped Goliath wouldn't be far away.

'All the way to the end and turn left,' said the second fly, 'but don't blame us, OK?'

Limpy was grateful for the directions, but a bit worried about why the flies seemed so awkward giving them.

'Is there something you're not telling me?' he said.

'No,' said one of the flies.

'Not really,' said the other.

Limpy decided not to waste any more time. Dad often said when he was milking stick insects that it was like trying to get information out of a fly.

'Thanks,' he said to the flies and the mosquito.

'You're welcome,' said the mosquito. 'Be careful. Don't let anyone with a frying pan creep up behind you.'

Limpy decided the mosquito meant well.

He headed off down the street without eating it.

16

The street was still busy and Limpy had to watch out for unfriendly human feet and tyres.

He tried not to look at the cooking show audience's poor chucked-away cane toad toys lying squashed on the road.

Limpy sighed. So much for going on TV and winning the hearts of humans.

At least the toys gave him a bit of camouflage. Each time Limpy felt human eyes glaring at him, he flopped down with his legs in the air and tried to look fluffy.

Finally he reached the end of the street and turned left.

Limpy felt lucky he had a sense of direction. A lot of cane toads didn't know left from right. Limpy had a little trick to help him remember. He reminded himself how when he was little, if things had been worse and the truck had squashed his leg completely, the one on the right would now be totally not right, and the one on the left would be the only one left.

Let's see, thought Limpy as he headed down the next street. When the flies said 'a bit further on', I wonder how far they meant?

He kept his eyes open for Penny and Goliath.

Then he saw Penny.

'Stack me,' he gasped.

At first Limpy thought his brains were still scrambled from the whizzing machine. Then he realised this must be what the flies had been trying to warn him about.

Inside the big shop window there was only one thing for sale.

Penny.

But not just one Penny.

A mountain of Pennys. All carefully stacked so their rows of big dark eyes stared out into the street and their piles of zip-up pockets and plastic straps gleamed in the sunlight.

'Penny,' came a miserable wail.

For a moment Limpy thought the wail was coming from the rows of yellow beaks in the shop window.

Then with a jolt he recognised the voice.

He peered around, trying to see Goliath.

Goliath was hopping slowly towards him from the opposite direction. His shoulders were slumped, a weary love-warrior despairing of ever seeing his beloved again.

And he mustn't, thought Limpy.

If Goliath caught sight of that shop window, Limpy shuddered to think what would happen.

Wild greed, probably, involving the smashing of large panes of glass and some nasty cuts to the warts. Then deep misery when Goliath realised his beloved was being produced in a factory in larger numbers than he could ever personally go out with, and that at least some of them would probably end up with other boyfriends.

Limpy imagined Goliath lumbering around the city with a bunch of flowers in each fist and a crazed look in his eye. Until the human army brought in snipers. Or maybe cricketers.

That mustn't happen.

Limpy knew what he had to do.

'Goliath,' he yelled, hopping urgently towards his cousin.

Goliath blinked and looked at Limpy, but not with his usual grin.

'You're going the wrong way,' said Limpy. 'This way.'

Before Goliath could get a glimpse into the shop window, Limpy steered him into a laneway that ran along the side of the shop.

'Is Penny down here?' said Goliath, his face brightening.

'Um,' said Limpy. 'Maybe.'

He hated lying to his cousin. He'd only ever done it once before, when Goliath asked him who invented sticks. Limpy said it might have been Goliath's father, who Goliath had never met.

Goliath had really liked that answer, and Limpy could see he really liked this one.

'Penny,' yelled Goliath excitedly, flinging himself along the laneway.

He hopped past a dumpster bin, glancing into it, then scrambled to a stop and turned back and clambered into the bin.

Limpy hurried over.

Goliath had disappeared. But Limpy could see exactly where he was. Rubbish and cardboard boxes were flying into the air.

Cardboard boxes, Limpy saw with concern, with pictures of Penny on them.

'Penny,' croaked Goliath's voice.

Limpy feared that Goliath was about to discover how busy the Penny factory was these days. Good news for the factory, heartbreak for Goliath.

But when Goliath appeared, his face was ecstatic and his arm was round a familiar yellow-beaked fully insulated plastic figure.

'Penny,' he whispered, gazing into her big penguin eyes.

He clambered out of the bin, clasping his beloved to his chest, and stroked her straps.

'Look, Limpy,' he said, his eyes wide with joy and wonder. 'It's Penny.'

Well, thought Limpy sadly, a Penny.

Goliath's smile turned into a scowl.

'That brute of a human child,' he said. 'Dumping my love in the garbage. And look, that monster broke her zip.'

Limpy saw that the toggle was missing from one of Penny's zips. Which probably explained why the shop had put her in the bin.

Goliath was rummaging around inside Penny's pockets.

'And,' he said, outraged, 'the greedy little mongrel ate all our cheese sticks.'

In Penny's pockets, Limpy saw, were just white beads of industrial packing material. For a fleeting hopeful moment, Limpy wondered if this might be when Goliath started to go off Penny.

But Goliath popped some of the packing material into his mouth and seemed to quite like it.

'Never mind, darling,' he cooed into one of Penny's plastic ears. 'We're back together and we'll never be parted again.'

Limpy wanted to feel happy for Goliath. He did in a sort of way. But something inside him didn't feel right. It was the sharp pang he got when he was even a little bit dishonest.

Should he tell Goliath about the other Pennys?

No, Limpy said to himself. That would be selfish. I'd be causing Goliath pain just to make myself feel better. Plus he might turn into a jealousy-crazed monster. Best not to tell him. Let him live with a little lie.

Limpy felt a big grateful muscly arm crushing

his shoulders and slobbery grateful lips kissing his head.

'I'll never be able to thank you enough, Limpy,' said Goliath. 'You found Penny. You're an angel.'

Limpy's crook leg started to twitch.

A lot.

'Storm's coming,' he said to Goliath. 'A big one. We'd better get back to the TV studio.'

He dragged Goliath and Penny along the lane, away from the shop.

Goliath was frowning.

'Why don't we just go home?' he said.

'Because,' said Limpy, 'there's still a chance we can do what we came here to do. If the TV chef is still at the studio and if we can get her to taste some Toad Delight, there's still a chance cane toads everywhere can live in peace and safety.'

Goliath didn't say anything.

Which was, Limpy realised, because he wasn't even listening.

They'd come to the end of the laneway, and Goliath was staring at something across the road.

A grassy oval behind a metal fence. Lots of human children running around. The children were wearing a kind of uniform, and Limpy wondered for a nervous moment if this was a human army battalion for younger soldiers.

He didn't think so.

The children were running around very happily and they reminded Limpy of young cane toads playing at the swamp academy at home.

This must be a school.

Goliath suddenly rushed across the road towards the fence, not looking either way for traffic.

'Goliath,' yelled Limpy, following anxiously. 'Where are you going?'

Goliath stopped at the fence.

He stood there, one arm round Penny, his other hand gripping a metal fence post, and his whole body trembling.

He was staring across the oval at something.

'What is it?' said Limpy, peering in the same direction.

Goliath gave a wail of disbelief.

Limpy saw what it was.

On the other side of the oval was a school building. On the verandah, hanging from hooks, were lots and lots of Pennys.

17

Before Limpy could stop him, Goliath squeezed between the fence posts and started hopping frantically across the oval.

'Come back,' yelled Limpy.

Goliath ignored him. And ignored the human children too. Just kept going straight towards the row of Pennys.

The children were too busy with their games to notice Goliath. Plus Goliath was mostly covered by his own Penny, so a child glancing over would just think an insulated lunch bag was being blown around in the strong wind that was springing up.

That's what Limpy hoped.

He squeezed through the fence and went after Goliath.

Some camouflage of his own would have been good. A Penny or a couple of fluffy cane toad toys. But the only places for him to catch his breath were a few clumps of long grass.

Limpy finally made it to the verandah in one piece and only slightly grazed by a passing football.

Goliath was already there, in a frenzy.

He was jumping up, trying to grab the straps of the Pennys and haul them off the hooks.

'Limpy,' he panted. 'Help me. There's been a tragic mix-up. We've got to get all these Pennys home so I can work out which is the real one.'

Limpy wondered how to break it to Goliath that they couldn't do that.

Goliath didn't seem to have noticed that all the bags had personal things on them. Stickers and charm bracelets and footy club keyrings. And each bag had a different squiggly line on it.

Limpy wasn't totally sure what the squiggles were, but he was fairly certain they were names.

'We need transport,' said Goliath. 'I'll grab the Pennys, you get a truck.'

Limpy opened his mouth to try to calm Goliath down, but before he could, his leg started twitching again, more than it ever had before.

It didn't stop.

Limpy looked at the sky.

A rim of darkness was growing on the horizon. He'd never seen anything like it. It was darker than the darkest bushfire smoke. Even darker than the vast swarm of flying insects he sometimes saw trying to get away from Goliath at lunchtime.

Limpy peered anxiously at the oval.

The children were all still playing.

If this storm has hail, thought Limpy, these kids will be history.

He hopped up and down and waved his arms.

'Storm,' he yelled at the kids. 'Get under cover.'

The children ignored him. Didn't even hear him probably. Limpy knew he wasn't croaking loud enough, not in this wind. Goliath always said cars shouldn't be the only ones with horns. Right now, Limpy agreed.

Lightning flashed in the distance.

Thunder shook the air, getting closer.

Limpy wondered if he should go and find a human teacher and spray them, just on their shoes, to get their attention.

No need.

An adult human appeared on the verandah and pressed a button on the wall. A loud bell rang several times. The children all stopped and turned, then started running towards the building.

Limpy was relieved.

Until he remembered Goliath.

Several bags were now off their hooks and lying on the verandah. Goliath's warts were bulging with effort as he tried to drag them away.

'Leave them,' said Limpy. 'Come on, we've got to hide.'

Too late.

Human feet were all around them. A swarm of school shoes with rippled soles that looked even tougher than the skin on Goliath's neck. Sometimes when Goliath was eating razor clams one or two tried to escape sideways, but they never made it through.

Limpy tried to grab Goliath so they could escape sideways, but there were too many feet and Goliath was tangled up in the straps of too many bags.

Hopeless, thought Limpy. When the kids realise Goliath is trying to steal their bags, those rippled school shoes will become merciless weapons.

Limpy said a silent goodbye to Mum and Dad and Charm, and apologised for not making a difference.

I should have been able to, he said to them. With a storm-warning leg and Toad Delight, I should have been able to make a big difference.

He closed his eyes and waited to be trampled. Or if not that, torn apart by the storm.

But instead he was gently picked up.

Limpy opened his eyes. And blinked.

Friendly laughing faces all around him. Human children, happy to see him. Limpy wondered which ones were the squiggles.

Then he noticed something else amazing. The children seemed delighted by Goliath's attempts to steal their bags.

The wind was blowing hard and cold now. The verandah shuddered with thunder. More human adults appeared and clapped their hands. Limpy guessed they were teachers. The kids grabbed the bags, and Goliath, and they all went inside.

Stack me, thought Limpy as he found himself carried into a classroom. Of course. That's why the children are so happy to see us. They think we were trying to save their bags from the storm.

It was a huge storm.

The teachers made the kids pull the desks away from the windows and put them all in the middle of the room. Then everyone huddled under them.

Humans and cane toads.

The wind howled. Hail crashed against the windows. Tree branches did cartwheels across the oval. The metal roof of the school screeched like a galah Limpy knew with a really bad singing voice.

A girl cuddled Limpy.

It was very kind of her because he was starting to feel a bit scared. He'd just noticed that the roof of the school didn't have a single hookworm holding it together.

'Don't be frightened,' the girl whispered. 'It's just Mr Weather being grouchy. We've learned how Mr Weather gets cross sometimes. Mostly because accelerating non-renewable energy transfers are permanently altering carbon dioxide ratios.'

Limpy didn't have a clue what she was saying, but she was saying it in such a gentle friendly voice that he was sure it was something nice.

'Next week,' the girl said, 'for homework, we're going to think of ways to cheer Mr Weather up. Probably by dismantling the fossil fuel industry and forcing politicians to get real.'

Limpy could have listened to her soft caring voice all afternoon, but he was worried about Goliath.

Under the next desk, Goliath was sitting with a group of boys.

The boys were chatting to him. Limpy guessed it was to keep their spirits up. But Goliath wasn't listening. He was deep in thought, his arm round his dumpster Penny, staring at all the other Pennys strewn around the room.

Poor Goliath, thought Limpy. After this painful experience, he'll probably never want to risk falling in love ever again.

Thunder suddenly crashed so loudly, Limpy assumed it didn't think Goliath would either.

Some of the children were looking frightened and miserable and almost as unhappy as Goliath. Some of them were doing the wet thing with their eyes. The teachers were going from child to child, hugging them and talking to them softly and drying their faces.

Their kindness reminded Limpy of Mum, and he wished that more of the drivers on the highway at home could be teachers.

Finally, after a lot more howling wind and scary tree damage and even scarier galah karaoke, the storm blew over.

One of the teachers opened a door and peered outside, then said something and all the children came out from under the desks.

The girl put Limpy down on top of a desk and hurried away. He tried to see where she'd gone, to thank her for looking after him, but he couldn't.

A boy put Goliath onto the desk next to Limpy.

Goliath was still holding onto Penny.

'Are you OK?' said Limpy.

Goliath sighed.

'I'm an idiot,' he said, looking sadly at his Penny.

'No, you're not,' said Limpy. 'You fell in love. That's not being an idiot.'

'I'm not talking about falling in love,' said Goliath. 'I'm talking about what I'm feeling now. How I'm really glad I've got Penny, but I can't stop thinking about all the Pennys I haven't got.'

Oh dear, thought Limpy. That is a problem.

'So I've decided,' said Goliath, 'that I've got a lot more to learn about being in love, particularly where cheese sticks are involved.'

Before Limpy could say anything, there was a commotion near one of the doorways.

Limpy peered across the classroom.

The girl who'd been looking after him had just been outside. She was back inside now, and she was doing the wet thing with her eyes, a lot.

Limpy saw why.

She was holding the remains of a Penny. It must have been left out in the storm. It was sodden and shredded to ribbons by the wind and the hail.

Limpy wished he could do something to help her feel better. Like she had for him.

He had a wild thought. Would Goliath ever consider selling his frothy dribble to a human fast-food company and using the money to buy the girl a new Penny?

No, probably not. All those times at home when the family had asked Goliath to share something. The protests. The tantrums. The stuffing everything into his mouth. Beetles. Worms. Sticks. Then pretending his jaws had got jammed so he couldn't open them again.

No, dopey idea.

Limpy was trying to think of some other way to help the girl, when he heard a thud.

Goliath had dropped onto the floor and was hopping over to her. Carrying his Penny.

He stopped in front of the girl.

He looked at his Penny for a long time. Gave it a long hug.

Then laid it gently at the girl's feet.

18

It was dark when they arrived back at the TV studio.

They would have got there earlier, but they had to hide for a while in a front garden after a car tried to drive over them in a side street.

Limpy was worried Goliath would jump out of the prickle bush and yell at the car, and that the driver would see him in the rear-vision mirror and turn the car around and have another go.

But Goliath just watched the car speed away down the street.

'Might not be a vicious killer,' he murmured. 'Might just be feeling a bit grumpy cos his heart got broken when love went wrong.'

Limpy pulled some prickles out of Goliath's shoulders to clear a patch big enough to give him a hug.

'Once they've had a proper taste of Toad Delight,' said Limpy, 'I don't reckon any human will stay grumpy for long.'

As the two of them got closer to the studio, Limpy wondered if the whole place would be shut tighter than Goliath's bulging mouth in the old days, back when he was greedy and selfish.

But like Goliath's generous heart today, the studio was still open.

At least, Limpy saw, a drain cover was.

He and Goliath wriggled along inside a slimy pipe that Limpy hoped would lead into the studio.

'Yum,' murmured Goliath.

Limpy was pleased that Goliath was having a snack. It had been a long day and a long hop back to the studio. Limpy would have nibbled some slime himself if he wasn't feeling too anxious to eat.

Too full of hopes and wishes.

Please, he whispered silently to the universe, or at least the part of it that was in the drainpipe. Please let the cooking show chef still be here. Please let her agree to taste some fresh frothy dribble and discover the deliciousness of Toad Delight. And please let humans be grateful that cane toads are happy to share it with them for ever.

A mighty rumble echoed along the pipe.

For a moment Limpy thought it was the universe answering.

'Sorry,' said Goliath.

'That's OK,' said Limpy, a bit disappointed.

If it had been the universe replying, he could have asked it why the weather was being so unfriendly these days.

After a while they reached the end of the pipe. It had mesh across it, blocking their exit.

Goliath, perked up by his snack, thumped the mesh until it popped off.

'Good on you,' said Limpy.

They wriggled out into a big room with puddles of water on the floor.

Parked there were the four-wheel drives that had brought them from the swamp. The vehicles both had water dripping off them.

'I think they've just been washed,' said Limpy. 'Which means probably some of the cooking show humans are still here.'

Goliath was looking worried.

'Do we have to go back into that studio again?' he said. 'Last time we barely got away from there with our buttocks in one piece.'

Limpy sighed.

Goliath was brave and kind and generous, but sometimes he needed things explained a few times.

Limpy stood on tiptoe and put his hands on Goliath's big shoulders.

'You and Penny did something wonderful today,' he said. 'Thanks to you, there's a girl who knows how kind and generous cane toads can be.'

'And all her classmates,' said Goliath. 'They know too.'

'Yes,' said Limpy. 'They do. And it's a great start. But we want all humans to know that. And with the help of your frothy dribble, they will.'

Goliath thought about this. His big face lit up with pride. Then he paused.

'Does that mean I have to be whizzed around again?' he said.

Limpy nodded.

'In that machine?' said Goliath.

Limpy nodded again.

Goliath grinned.

'Hooray,' he said. 'Dribble city. Let's do it.'

The lights were on in the corridor leading from the vehicle-washing room, and before Limpy was very far along it, he recognised it as the corridor that led to the TV cooking show studio.

'We're in luck,' he whispered to Goliath.

'Stick with me,' said Goliath. 'I've got lucky warts.'

When Limpy saw that the studio door was open a crack, and lights were on inside, he had to agree.

But once they'd hopped into the studio, Limpy felt their luck running out.

There were no humans to be seen.

Not the chef, or her production assistants. Not even any cleaners who might be prepared to take a break and taste a bit of Toad Delight.

The studio was empty.

Then Limpy heard the buzz of voices in the distance.

He peered around and saw a small group over on the cooking show set.

Not humans.

Insects.

Limpy hopped over to them, Goliath at his side. A familiar voice was speaking.

'Very disappointing,' the mosquito was saying to the two flies. 'Just goes to show, in this cooking game, never listen to rumours. Or ants. Specially not dopey ants who reckon that cane toad frothy dribble is the best thing they've ever tasted. Frankly, I think it's revolting.'

Limpy saw that the mosquito and the two flies were tasting old frothy dribble they'd scraped off the kitchen bench.

Frothy dribble that was very hard and very dry and not frothy.

'Excuse me,' said Limpy.

The mosquito glanced up, saw Limpy and looked like it had just been sprayed.

'Oh no,' it said. 'I am so embarrassed. Please forgive me. I shouldn't have said any of those terrible things. I should have waited till I could post them online anonymously.'

'It's OK,' said Limpy. 'But if you want to try Toad Delight, you should try it fresh.'

'Fresh frothy dribble?' said the mosquito.

'Yes,' said Limpy.

'Yes,' said Goliath.

'Yum,' said the flies.

But Limpy could see there was a problem. The whizzing machine wasn't there. The chef must have packed it away.

'Is the chef around anywhere?' Limpy asked the insects hopefully.

The flies chortled.

'She's been fired,' said the mosquito. 'The network's looking for a replacement. I offered, but you know how it is.'

Limpy felt a bit bad. The TV chef had probably lost her job because of the frothy dribble chaos in the studio. But then Limpy remembered she'd sliced the buttocks off quite a few cane toads, so he didn't feel very sorry for her.

He concentrated on the task at hand.

This news was a setback but not a disaster. A new TV chef would be hired soon. Best to have some fresh Toad Delight ready and waiting.

'Is there anything here that's flat and slippery?' said Limpy.

The mosquito pointed to a room at the back of the set. Limpy went to investigate.

Amazing. Stored in the room was all the food used on the cooking show. Shelves and cupboards and boxes and baskets and fridges and freezers, all full of food.

Limpy heard a strangled squeak behind him.

It was Goliath, looking around the room. His eyes were bulging and his tongue was quivering.

'Not yet,' said Limpy. 'We'll do the dribble first, then you can have a snack.'

Goliath agreed. With only a couple of small grumbles. And one very small tantrum.

Limpy found a pack of salami slices. Goliath ripped it open, but before he could start eating it Limpy pulled a slice out of the packet and carefully placed it on the kitchen bench.

'Sit on it with your knees under your chin,' said Limpy.

Goliath did.

'Ow,' he said.

'What?' said Limpy.

'It's got chilli in it,' said Goliath.

'We'll be quick,' said Limpy.

He grabbed Goliath's arm and started running. He spun Goliath around faster and faster. Limpy had never run so fast.

For the first time in his life, he was glad his crook leg made him run in circles. He was whizzing around now, and so was Goliath.

But so far, no frothy dribble.

Please, begged Limpy silently. Frothy dribble. We need you.

Limpy's plea was answered when a big gob of frothy dribble slopped him in the face. He kept whizzing round for a while longer, then slowed down until he and Goliath came to a stop.

All that was moving was the frothy dribble dripping off both their chins.

Limpy didn't hesitate. He slurped a big mouthful. So did Goliath. And the mosquito and the two flies. They all looked at each other, all swooshing it around their mouths and smacking their lips.

None of the others looked happy.

Limpy sagged.

This frothy dribble didn't taste anything like the stuff he'd tasted by the highway. It wasn't sweet, or tangy, or full of yummy flavours. It was ordinary. Bland. It tasted like dribble, just a bit frothier.

'Ordinary,' said the mosquito.

'Bland,' said one of the flies.

'Just dribble,' said the other one.

'I don't get it,' said Goliath. 'Unless . . . maybe your frothy dribble only goes delicious when you're in love.'

Limpy frowned. That didn't seem likely. Mum and Dad were in love, but ants had never hurled themselves at their dribble.

'Maybe it's something to do with those bike vehicles,' said Limpy. 'Or the stretchy clothes humans wear when they ride them. Goliath, when you were whizzing round on the bike, did you put anything into your mouth?'

Limpy knew it was unlikely, but possible.

'Life's full of mysteries, isn't it, young fella?' said a voice behind him.

Limpy's warts went cold.

He turned.

The dog from the TV crew was standing very close, looking at Limpy with a very grim expression that included quite a lot of teeth.

'For example,' said the dog, 'it was a mystery to me why you disappeared when we had a deal.'

Limpy didn't know what to say.

The dog's teeth looked even bigger and sharper than before.

'Oh well,' said the dog. 'Things move fast in the TV industry. The network has got a new weather man who uses science instead of crook legs. And they've decided not to do another cooking show for a while. So I'm sure you two won't mind hopping back into the cage.'

Limpy didn't like the sound of that. Goliath clearly didn't either.

'You're not taking me, you mongrel,' he yelled.

Goliath leaped off the bench and disappeared into the food storage room. He reappeared gripping a large stick and headed towards the dog in a menacing way.

'You're not taking my cousin either, fleabag,' growled Goliath.

Oh no, thought Limpy. If Goliath tries to whack the dog, we're goners. Instead of solving the Toad Delight mystery, we'll end up with blue heels after all. Because we'll be dead.

Goliath took a few more menacing steps.

The dog drew itself up to its full height, which was high, and bared its teeth, which were definitely big. And sharp.

Goliath stopped. He sniffed the stick.

'Hang on,' he said.

He gave the stick a lick.

'I've tasted this before,' he said. 'Delicious.'

The mosquito and the flies buzzed over and tasted the stick too.

'It is delicious,' said the mosquito. 'Sweet and tangy and full of yummy flavours. But then sugar cane always is.'

Limpy stared at the stick.

He recognised it now. Exactly the same type of green stick as the one Goliath had found by the side of the highway and jammed into the wheel of the human's bike. The same type of stick Goliath had been hanging onto when he first gave the world Toad Delight.

Sugar cane.

It didn't grow in the swamp, but sometimes it fell off passing cane trucks.

Stack me, thought Limpy, sagging with weary disappointment. Frothy dribble isn't Toad Delight after all.

It's Sugar Cane Delight.

Goliath was staring at the stick of sugar cane too. It was hanging loosely in his hand, not even a tiny bit menacing.

'Oops,' he said miserably. 'I think we've made a bit of a mistake.'

Limpy didn't reply.

It was all too overwhelming and crushing and awful.

The best chance cane toads had ever had to win the affection and love of humans, gone, finished, never even existed.

'Cheer up,' said the dog. 'It's not all bad news. Tomorrow I start work on a brand-new series.'

'Congratulations,' said Limpy weakly.

'With both of you, if you want,' said the dog to Limpy and Goliath. 'It's a new science show. The producer wants to do the first one on cane toads. Film them in their natural habitat, doing what cane toads do. Tomorrow morning we're going back to your swamp. Thought you blokes might like the chance to tag along, tell your folks to be on their best behaviour. All you've got to do is hop into the cage and leave the rest to us.'

Limpy stared at the dog.

Was this true? Was it a genuine offer? Or a cruel piece of trickery and revenge? For all Limpy knew, the network could be planning a new handicraft series. Episode one. Cane toad placemats.

'It's a win-win situation,' said the dog. 'You get to go home and we get good shots of cane toads who don't mind us being close and personal with the camera.'

'Very good plan,' said the mosquito to the dog. 'I reckon you'll be an executive producer after this.'

Limpy's head was spinning.

Should he grab Goliath and run for it, or take a chance?

'Well?' said the dog.

Limpy looked at Goliath and saw that Goliath was thinking the same thing as him. This was their last chance to make a difference.

Goliath put his arm round Limpy's shoulders and looked squarely at the dog.

'Just one question we need you to answer,' said Goliath.

'What's that?' said the dog.

'Will we get grasshoppers?' said Goliath.

Limpy sighed.

The dog ignored Goliath.

'What's your decision?' said the dog to Limpy. 'Last chance.'

Limpy took a deep breath.

'Put us in the cage,' he said.

19

The dog was telling the truth. Limpy could hardly speak, he was so relieved.

So relieved, and so nervous.

This was their last chance.

Things had to happen here in the swamp today that had never happened before.

'Thank goodness,' said Mum, hugging Limpy and Goliath. 'Thank goodness you're alright.'

She and Dad and Charm were glowing with delight, but Limpy could tell they were nervous too, about the TV crew being back.

While the humans unloaded their gear and set up the camera, Limpy took Mum and Dad and Charm and some of the other cane toads to one side for a chat.

'They want to film us in our natural habitat,' he explained. 'Doing what we usually do.'

'You know the sort of thing,' said Goliath. 'Stuffing aphids into ants and then stuffing the ants into beetles and then stuffing the beetles into slugs and then marinating them.'

Limpy sighed.

Goliath seemed to have forgotten the long talk they'd had in the cage last night. The one where Goliath had promised not to put more than one species at a time into his mouth in front of the cameras. Or anything at all into his bottom.

Limpy looked at the serious faces around him, all waiting to hear what he was going to say next.

This won't be easy, he thought. Persuading everyone to do the opposite of what we usually do.

Mum was looking thoughtful.

'I reckon,' she said, 'we should do the opposite of what we usually do. Not stuff ourselves. Not be greedy. I reckon that would make a nice change.'

Limpy stared at Mum.

'That's right,' he said weakly.

'We were talking about it yesterday,' said Dad. 'Another big storm hit and we were in the poo because you were away and we'd eaten all the storm beetles.'

'And not just storm beetles,' said Charm. 'You know how the leaf-bug-gobbling march flies used to keep the leaf bug numbers under control?'

Limpy nodded.

'We ate the last few leaf-bug-gobbling march flies a couple of days ago,' said Charm.

She pointed up into the trees.

Limpy stared. The leaves were covered with leaf bugs.

'It's not our fault,' said one of the leaf bugs. 'We're uncomfortable with this too.'

'You were right, Limpy,' said Charm. 'What you said before you went away. We've been greedy and things need to change.'

Limpy wanted to give her a hug, but there was too much to do.

The dog came over.

'Camera's ready,' it said. 'Let's get started.'

'Standing by,' said Limpy.

The humans moved closer with the camera.

'Of course,' said a loud voice nearby, 'I can fit heaps of those leaf bugs into my mouth if I want to. Probably more if I spit my chewing gum out first.'

Limpy turned round.

Goliath was sitting against a tree with his arm round a camera bag.

'Goliath,' hissed Limpy.

'Sorry,' said Goliath, pushing the bag away.

'Action! yelled the human director.

Limpy didn't understand the word, but he could tell by the way the human holding the camera crouched down low and put the camera very close to him that it was time to be nice.

'Charm,' he said. 'Would you like an ant?'

He held one out to her.

'Just a leg, thanks,' said Charm. 'So there's some left for the others.'

'Oh, go on,' said the ant. 'Have two legs at least or you'll be starving by lunchtime.'

'Dad and I will share a leg,' said Mum.

'Will we?' said Dad. 'Oh yes, right.'

'Do you have a preference?' Mum said to the ant. 'About which leg we take?'

'You choose,' said the ant. 'I'm hopeless at decisions.'

While Mum and Dad and Charm and Goliath shared the ant, and the ant's farewell words were to compliment them on their self-control and lack of greed, Limpy looked around.

All over the swamp, cane toads were saying 'after you', and 'I couldn't possibly', and 'why don't we parcel up these slime borers for the hungry toads overseas?'.

Yes, thought Limpy. At last we're showing our good sides. When humans see this on TV, things will start to change at last.

He glanced at the human director, to see if the director had noticed how Goliath hadn't eaten a single leaf bug yet. Limpy hoped they'd already got the shot of Goliath showing restraint, because if Goliath didn't have a leaf bug soon, his warts would probably pop.

The human director didn't look happy.

Neither did the dog.

Oh no, thought Limpy. What's wrong? Has one of our lot chewed a cable or something?

The dog came over.

'This isn't going so well,' said the dog. 'Why aren't you guys eating more?'

'We're fine, honest,' said Limpy. 'We're not big eaters, not really.'

He could see the dog didn't believe him.

'Here's the situation,' said the dog. 'We came out here to film you lot stuffing yourselves senseless with bugs.'

Limpy stared at the dog.

It was what he'd feared all along.

'I know what you're thinking,' said the dog, 'and it's not that. If we wanted to make you toads look bad, we'd just give your cousin an old car and let him eat the seats.'

'So what do you want?' said Limpy.

The dog glanced around to make sure they weren't being overheard.

'Don't tell any other species,' said the dog, 'but humans are in trouble. Too many cars, too many power stations, humans and the weather aren't getting on. While they work out how to fix the friendship, they need leaves.'

Limpy blinked.

'Leaves?' he said. 'Leaves off branches and stuff? That's easy. We can give them lots of leaves. Gum leaves, fig leaves, stink leaves. Truckloads of them.'

'They need leaves that are still growing on trees,' said the dog. 'It's complicated, but leaves on trees do things that makes the weather very happy.'

Limpy nodded.

Probably something to do with how leaves tickle you or something.

126

Then Limpy remembered the leaf bugs. He looked up. Every leaf in the canopy of branches above their heads had a leaf bug on it, trying hard not to chew. They weren't doing a very good job. The leaves had so many holes in them they looked like green mosquito nets.

'It's not our fault,' said one of the leaf bugs. 'We're just not used to being left up here for so long.'

'It's unnatural,' said another.

'Eat and then be eaten,' said a third. 'That's our philosophy.'

Limpy looked at the dog again.

'On this show,' said the dog, 'our viewers want to see leaves being protected. Which means leaf bugs being eaten. Lots of them.'

'Hear, hear,' said the leaf bugs.

Limpy understood.

He imagined how grateful humans would be to a species who could do that. Who could be greedy, just sometimes, for a good cause.

Oh how humans would cherish and value such a species. Be kind and polite to them. Not squash them flat on the highway

'Goliath,' called Limpy. 'Got a moment?'

20

The early-morning sun twinkled cheerfully through the swamp.

Limpy gave the sun a smile back.

The sun was right. Even though life had some sad parts, it wasn't a bad idea to start each day with a bit of cheerful twinkling.

Limpy hopped onto the highway and over to Uncle Spencer and Aunty Sasha.

'G'day, Uncle Spencer and Aunty Sasha,' he said. Time to get you stacked up, if that's alright with you.'

Uncle Spencer and Aunty Sasha didn't reply.

Limpy wasn't surprised.

The sun had baked Uncle Spencer and Aunty Sasha harder than overcooked pizzas, and Limpy knew from experience that overcooked pizzas didn't have a lot to say for themselves.

'Good news,' Limpy said. 'No new rellies squashed this morning.'

He was pretty sure Uncle Spencer and Aunty Sasha would be pleased to hear that.

'Third morning in a row,' said Limpy. 'Now that everyone's eating a bit less, there's enough food in the swamp and nobody needs to come to the highway for dinner. And when humans see Goliath on TV eating those leaf bugs and keeping nature in balance, they probably won't even come after us with cricket bats.'

Limpy paused. He'd just had a thought.

'Which means,' he said quietly to Uncle Spencer and Aunty Sasha, 'you're the last flat rellies. You probably don't feel quite as happy about that as I do, but it makes you very special.'

Limpy heaved Uncle Spencer and Aunty Sasha onto his back. He tottered to his room with them. Because he wanted them to feel special, he put them very carefully onto the very top of the uncle and aunty stacks.

Just as he finished, Charm came in.

'It's Goliath again,' she said. 'He wants to know if he can do a bit more leaf bug population control.'

Limpy rolled his eyes.

'I've told Goliath a hundred times,' he said. 'Once a month, not once an hour. And he probably won't need to do it again because the leaf-bug-gobbling march flies have started to come back, now that we're not eating so many of them.'

'I know,' said Charm. 'That's what I told him. Isn't it great?'

'Yes,' said Limpy. 'It is.'

'Do you think the humans will notice?' said Charm.

Limpy hesitated.

He'd been thinking about this a lot.

He was starting to wonder if he'd been a bit selfish when it came to humans. Thinking that cane toads were so important to them. When the entire poor human species was probably lying awake at night worrying about the hail dents in their cars and how to make friends with the weather.

'I'm starting to feel a bit like Goliath,' said Limpy. 'Goliath reckons he's got a lot more to learn about love, particularly where cheese sticks are involved. I'm starting to think I've got quite a lot more to learn about life, particularly where humans are involved.'

Charm looked at him, her little face glowing.

'I wish humans were more like you,' she said.

Mum and Dad came in.

'Guess what?' said Mum.

'We've just seen a couple of storm beetles,' said Dad.

'Thank you, Limpy,' said Mum.

Limpy felt a bit embarrassed by all the attention.

'We're proud of you, son,' said Dad.

He gave Limpy a hug.

Mum put her hand on Limpy's face and gently stroked his warts. It was something she used to do when he was little, and he still loved it.

'I was wrong, Limpy,' said Mum. 'What I said before. One cane toad can make a difference.'

'Two,' said an indignant voice.

Goliath came in, holding a big dollop of frothy dribble.

'I've been spinning myself around on some swamp slime,' he said. 'Do you think humans will like this? It's a secret recipe that involves me getting my tongue all the way into old soft drink cans.'

'Maybe one day,' said Limpy. 'But for now, why don't we see if the ants would like some?'

Mum and Dad both had their arms round him, and he put his round Goliath and Charm.

His warts tingled with love.

Frothy dribble has its uses, thought Limpy happily, but this is the real Toad Delight.

Join Limpy the cane toad in four hilarious, heroic adventures

From the Sydney Olympics to the Amazon jungle, Limpy just can't help getting into some sticky situations.

Be warned — it could get messy!

'A hilarious high-speed read . . . a real ripper!'
— Sunday Times

Bumface

His mum calls him Mr Dependable,
but Angus can barely cope. Another baby would
be a disaster. So Angus comes up with a bold and
brave plan to stop her getting pregnant.
That's when he meets Rindi.
And Angus thought *he* had problems . . .

Two Weeks With The Queen

'I need to see the Queen about my sick brother.'

Colin Mudford is on a quest. His brother is very ill and
the doctors in Australia don't seem to be able to cure
him. Colin reckons it's up to him to find the best doctor
in the world. And how better to do this than by asking
the Queen for help?

It all started with a Scarecrow

Puffin is well over sixty years old.
Sounds ancient, doesn't it? But Puffin has never been
so lively. We're always on the lookout for the next big
idea, which is how it began all those years ago.

Penguin Books was a big idea from the mind of
a man called Allen Lane, who in 1935 invented
the quality paperback and changed the world.
**And from great Penguins, great Puffins grew,
changing the face of children's books forever.**

The first four Puffin Picture Books were hatched in 1940 and the
first Puffin story book featured a man with broomstick arms called
Worzel Gummidge. In 1967 Kaye Webb, Puffin Editor, started the
Puffin Club, promising to **'make children into readers'.**
She kept that promise and over 200,000 children became
devoted Puffineers through their quarterly installments of
Puffin Post, which is now back for a new generation.

Many years from now, we hope you'll look back and
remember Puffin with a smile. **No matter what your age
or what you're into, there's a Puffin for everyone.**
The possibilities are endless, but one thing is for sure:
whether it's a picture book or a paperback, a sticker book
or a hardback, **if it's got that little Puffin
on it – it's bound to be good.**

TOAD DELIGHT

Morris Gleitzman grew up in England and went to live in Australia when he was sixteen. He worked as a frozen-chicken thawer, sugar-mill rolling-stock unhooker, fashion-industry trainee, department-store Santa, TV producer, newspaper columnist and screenwriter. Then he had a wonderful experience. He wrote a novel for young people. Now he's one of the bestselling children's authors in Australia. He lives in Brisbane and Sydney and visits Britain regularly. His many books include *Two Weeks with the Queen*, *Bumface*, *Boy Overboard* and *Once*.

Visit Morris at his website:
morrisgleitzman.com